"I'm yours...for the night," Garrett murmured.

Gently he tossed Shari on the bed, then followed her down to the opulent white silk sheets. The bedding was soft to the skin. Shari had only imagined such bliss—a stark contrast to her own sagging twin bed in her cramped Manhattan apartment. *This was heaven.*

Garrett was bearing down on her now, closing his mouth over one nipple, then the other. Slowly he began to kiss the length of her belly, to tease the concave surface of her navel. He blazed a trail of fire with his mouth, until she began to writhe and whimper.

This wasn't happening. Not with her fantasy man...

And it was only getting hotter. She was trembling by the time he parted her knees. Low masculine groans of hunger filled the room as he seared the tender skin of her thighs with wet kisses.

If he ever figured out who she was...

But he wouldn't find out. Shari squeezed her eyes shut, putting a shutter over the past. Enjoying this once-in-a-lifetime encounter was all that mattered.

No matter the price...

Dear Reader,

In 1999, Harlequin will celebrate its 50th anniversary in North America. Canadian publishing executive Richard Bonnycastle founded the company in 1949. Back then, they published a wide variety of American and British paperbacks—from mysteries and Westerns, to classics and cookbooks. In later years, the company focused on romance exclusively, and today Harlequin is the world's leading publisher of series romance fiction. Our books are sold in over one hundred countries and published in more than twenty-three languages. Love stories are a universal experience!

Harlequin Temptation is delighted to help celebrate this very special anniversary. We're throwing a bachelor auction...and you're invited! Join five of our leading authors as they put a sexy hero on the auction block. Sparks fly when the heroines get a chance to bid on their fantasy men.

Bestselling author Leandra Logan serves up a delicious hero, Garrett, and a resourceful heroine. Shari has never got over her crush on Garrett. One night with him will be the cure—or so she thinks. But the tables are turned when Garrett is suddenly in hot pursuit of Shari's alter ego, Flame! Leandra has written for Harlequin since 1990 and has over twenty books to her credit. Look for a spin-off to *Just for the Night* in November 1999 featuring Shari's irascible brother, Dylan.

Each month we strive to bring you the very best stories and writers. And we plan to keep doing that for the next fifty years!

Happy Anniversary!

Birgit Davis-Todd
Senior Editor
Harlequin Temptation

Leandra Logan
JUST FOR THE NIGHT

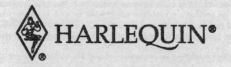

HARLEQUIN®

TORONTO • NEW YORK • LONDON
AMSTERDAM • PARIS • SYDNEY • HAMBURG
STOCKHOLM • ATHENS • TOKYO • MILAN • MADRID
PRAGUE • WARSAW • BUDAPEST • AUCKLAND

For Mary Anne Wilson
A California Girl Original!

ISBN 0-373-25825-9

JUST FOR THE NIGHT

1

THEY WOULD RUN OUT OF CASH before his turn on the auction block.

Garrett McNamara was on a certain course of doom, no question. There wouldn't be a single cent left in the place. Feminine groans, wistful, sympathetic, even slightly amused, would fill the perfumed air.

He could just imagine the headlines on tomorrow's society columns: Fire Sale Held At The Waldorf-Astoria. Bachelors Sold Off At Bargain Rates.

He'd be the laughingstock of his investment firm.

Rubbing his hands together, Garrett peered out between the curtains of the stage much like a frightened boy. The scene was the same one he'd spied upon intermittently over the past few hours, a crowd of formally dressed women seated at round banquet tables, armed with small evening bags and numbered paddles for bidding. Most of the bags hardly looked large enough to hold a checkbook or wallet. Did they take major credit cards?

He'd tried to pull out his credit card when they'd first approached him about this literacy fund-raiser. But the organizers had insisted he put his plastic away. Though they appreciated his generous offer, what they preferred was the loan of his gorgeous and eligible bachelor body for a thrilling evening of romance. It was their feeling invaluable publicity could be garnered from this kind of attention-grabbing stunt and would raise the most money over the long haul. Hard as he fumbled, he could think of no gracious way to decline. How cleverly they'd lured him in by putting such value on his person!

Since then, Garrett had swung from feelings of over-blown ego to outright terror. He'd ultimately settled his nerves by trying not to put much stock in the entire affair. It was bound to amount to nothing more than playing escort to some spoiled society waif, the kind who came a dime a dozen in Manhattan's finer clubs.

With these realistic scenarios playing through his mind, Garrett had arranged for his fantasy date to be a quick and immediate one, with lots of company to break the monotony. The highest bidder was in store for an evening of partying aboard his family's yacht, the *Temptation*.

Garrett was always comfortable aboard the lavish one-hundred-and-forty-nine-foot vessel. It had been in his family for years, purchased by his late father, Brent, back in the eighties to entertain his law firm's clients. Garrett and his mother, Gwen, used the boat as much as ever these days for both business and pleasure cruises.

Tonight's party was a bit of both. The guests would include Garrett's investment firm partners, their wives and Gwen, set to play the grande dame. Surely the event would meet auction standards: a glorious moonlight cruise in Atlantic waters with a stocked bar and brimming buffet, a dance band and contact with enough big shots for a lifetime's worth of name-dropping.

All the fancy trimmings of a magical night, with no emotional output necessary. Damn, he was brilliant.

Knowing his plan was set, however, did little to steady his final-hour nerves. Beneath all the glitter, being sold off like a side of beefcake seemed so primitive to Garrett. A man was supposed to do the hunting. To take the rules out of his hands seemed diabolical.

Perhaps he was being unfair, though. Garrett knew himself to be difficult, headstrong. He liked to be in charge of his affairs always, master of his universe. Why, he handled millions of dollars' worth of investments for his clients every day, was a millionaire in his own right many times over. This sort of event should be a piece of cake.

Again his original fear niggled him. He was number thirty-nine in the lineup of fifty bachelors. What if the bidding went flat?

"Mr. McNamara? Peekaboo."

He straightened up in a shot, letting the curtain fall back into place. "Mrs. Fontaine." He smiled down at the plump dowager in the tangerine chiffon gown. It seemed a sure bet she was assigned to him as a personal watchdog. Every time he tried to catch his breath, she was set squarely in his space.

"How you do roam." Her emerald ring glimmered under the stage lights as she wagged a finger beneath his nose.

He shifted his broad shoulders, ran a hand through his clipped jet hair. "It's been a long wait."

"Well, the waiting is over."

His expression softened boyishly. "They overextend themselves, run out of bidders?"

"And a sense of humor to boot!" She touched his black jacket sleeve, her glee fading as his chin trembled slightly. "Surely a catch like you isn't rattled by something as whimsical as this gala."

Garrett was lost for a fancy dodge, his worst fears spilling out. "This late in the game...guess I'd...you know...hate to find myself marked down to clearance."

"Nonsense!" Her bright eyes danced behind her spectacles as she scanned his tuxedoed form. "They've saved the best batch for last as far as I'm concerned, like bringing out the prime-cut filet mignon after the cornflakes."

Her bluntness took him aback. "Just what finishing school did you attend?"

"Your mother's," she crooned unashamedly. "We're sorority sisters."

"Wait until I tell her about this!"

"Now, who do you think recommended you for the auction in the first place?"

His handsome face lit up dangerously. Mother had played the innocent when he'd told her about this. She'd listened sympathetically to his venting, mildly pointed out that a worthy cause was involved, then, as if by inspiration, agreed to make the necessary arrangements for the yachting party and act as gracious hostess to whomever he escorted.

He should have known it was her right off. Gwen McNamara had a penchant for meddling in his affairs, had spent the past decade trying to set him up with one spoiled debutante or another. This would be right up her alley, giving a whole flock of women the chance to battle for him. Odds would be good that the winner would be suitable wife material in his mother's eyes, wealthy enough to dabble at a charitable affair and presumably sophisticated by her sheer wealth.

"Come along now, Garrett." One jeweled hand clamped down firmly on his wrist and the other set at the base of his spine, Mrs. Fontaine quickly had both of them in motion. The burly socialite missed her calling, Garrett decided. There had to be countless bars on the Lower East Side looking for fearless bouncers.

Moments later his name echoed over the sound system. "We're pleased to present our next bachelor on the bidding block. Manhattan financier Garrett McNamara!"

The call of the wild. Garrett thrust aside the curtain and launched onto the stage.

A round of applause rose as he strutted along the footlights. He gained polish and momentum, conceding that he did indeed look sharp in a dark tux, crisp white shirt and cummerbund. Had since his first formal function, the senior prom back at Brady High.

"Garrett is thirty years old," the auctioneer announced. "The McNamara of Crater, McNamara and Richtor Investments. He enjoys a woman with a sense of humor and playfulness. And does he ever want to play tonight, ladies. Your dream date would begin immediately, as a limousine is waiting to whisk you and a host of the rich and famous to Essex, Connecticut, for a romantic cruise aboard Garrett's own yacht, the *Temptation!* So if you've prepared yourself as the program suggested, with an overnight case full of essentials and some dancing shoes, jump right into the bidding."

Murmurs and applause swelled to Garrett's delight. The package sounded pretty good even to his own ears, surely as good as the others before him. He confidently gazed down into the dimly lit audience. Their lovely faces were upturned, mouths parted, scanning the skies like a nest of anxious birds waiting for a taste of raindrops.

Save for one nonchalant face.

A striking woman in red, seated front-row center, was spoiling the ego-pumping effect. She was in a world of her own, far too busy to clap or gush, forking a wedge of cheesecake between sips of ever-flowing champagne. Her hand lifted once, not to wave or point or make a premature bid, but to summon a hovering waiter holding a bottle of bubbly!

Garrett could not take his eyes off her as he moved and turned as instructed. Surely no taste of raindrops would satisfy her earthy kind of cravings. Watching her feed amused him, annoyed him, signaled a hunger in his own belly.

Talk about a fire sale. *She* was almost on fire, from her flowing copper hair to her beaded crimson gown, her body amazingly slender despite her hearty appetite.

He was on his final trip across the stage when she finally acknowledged his existence, raising her chin just a fraction for a full inspection that started at his shiny black shoes and traveled upward. It was a thorough, ever-so-casual flick of a stare, quick and singeing. She was so quickly back to her fork and food, he wasn't sure it happened at all.

Perhaps the lady in red was set there by Fate's strategic hand just to keep his soaring ego in check. The very idea brought a sweet, torturous strain to his fancy trousers. He was known for wanting what he couldn't have, dating way back.

Garrett pivoted on his heel rather sharply near the podium. If he didn't watch it, he'd be making a fool of himself. Surely she meant nothing in the grand scheme of the McNamara universe. She wouldn't want him, not with that attitude. By the way she was ogling and chowing down, she might have no interest in the bidding whatsoever but be on hand simply for the dinner and bachelor parade.

The auctioneer nodded approvingly then spoke up. "We'll start the bidding for Mr. McNamara at one thousand dollars...."

Paddles stirred the air around the tables for the next few minutes. The auctioneer didn't push it, taking her time as she'd done with the others, highlighting the unique points of interest of the dream date currently on the block.

Eventually, to Garrett's delight and amazement, the

bid was up to twenty-nine thousand dollars. Called once, twice.

"Make that an even thirty grand."

The proceedings were interrupted in the last instant before the gavel fell, not with a designated paddle but a fork licked clean of cheesecake.

"Sold!" the auctioneer called out gaily with a smack of wood. "To the lady in red!"

The lady in red? Garrett blinked into the bright stage lights. There was no mistake, the showy bid had come from the table of fire. She was milking the moment for all it was worth, too, carefully setting down her utensil, leisurely lifting her paddle to reveal her bidding number.

What a wildly impulsive thing to do, he marveled. Or was it calculatingly wild, all part of a preconceived plan to appear impulsive? There actually was an overnight bag, presumably "full of essentials," nudged against her chair. She was ready to be whisked away on a moment's notice, as he'd specified.

She'd come to win. She'd come for *him.*

But on what motivation? Was she a total stranger, or someone standing in the shadows of his daily routine, like a dazzled clerk from his company or a fitness nut from his health club? Surely he would recognize her from any previous encounter, no matter how minor, with that oversize sweet tooth, major attitude and thirty grand to spend.

Incredible, he was bought and paid for by a provocative mystery woman—and liking it! Instantly he began to regret surrounding himself with so many people tonight, tossing her into a business-social event like the average guest.

Why had he done something so stupid? Oh, yes, to avoid all threat of intimate contact. Ironically, a heat was already growing in the pit of his belly. It wasn't every day that a man met a woman who could turn him on so completely with as little as a look and a fork. If only he could change the itinerary, snatch her up and escape for a cozier evening. But he couldn't. Garrett had an ingrained sense of duty set in place by his affluent parents. One kept one's commitments, no matter how inconvenient.

But that didn't mean he couldn't have a bit of fun in the process, he decided. Somehow he'd work around all the people he'd armed himself with, uncover the mysteries surrounding this beauty.

The auctioneer was tapping her gavel on the podium to get some order. She was having little luck, as the room was humming excitedly over the fevered bidding, apparently unexpected this late into the event.

It was Garrett who ultimately brought a hush to the room by clearing his throat at the podium microphone. With a crook of his lips and finger, he spoke up silkily.

"Time to go…Red."

The lady in red was in the process of writing out her check with a flourish of pen. It appeared to be a larger-size bank draft, which she waved in the air, then with a sultry pucker blew on, supposedly to dry the ink. The sexy gesture brought fresh squeals and applause.

Garrett was ushered off the stage by Mrs. Fontaine and another formally dressed dowager. "We had such a time getting him out here in the first place," Mrs Fontaine chortled to the avid spectators. "Who'd believe it now!"

Garrett himself didn't believe it. But it was truly happening.

He soon discovered that his free-spending admirer had beat him backstage and was busily paying the clerk seated at a table.

Curious and desirous way beyond his usual limits, he

had to summon all his self-control to move closer in little more than a lazy saunter. Nearly a foot taller than she was, he had no trouble gazing over her bared shoulders to glance at her check and the receipt. Both bore the name Flame Unlimited.

He rolled the alias, steeped in innuendo, over in his mind with wry humor. Was it all part of the setup, looking like fire, acting like fire, setting him on fire?

He took a breath, hoping to calm himself. Incredibly, her scent, a zesty blend of perfumed body heat, only managed to fog his brain all the more.

Throughout his tailspin of feeling, *Flame* seemed oblivious to it all.

To the contrary, *Flame* was keenly aware of everything: Garrett's approach; his backfield inspection; his deep intake of breath, which threatened to swallow her whole. Finally, he was feeling the electricity that she believed had always existed between them.

Sweet and sexy déjà vu. It made her body swell under her tight beaded gown. Ah, yes, exactly what she was after, exactly what she was paying for!

Ooh, but the cost of this indulgence was steeper than she ever imagined. The receipt in her hand held the staggering figure of thirty thousand dollars. A fortune dropped with the lift of a dessert fork. *Thirty thousand dollars.* Just for the night.

Like a tiny teakettle on the boil, last-minute doubts bubbled to the surface of her saucy faux persona. Would he recognize her at close range? Realize that she was his boyhood pal Dylan's little sister, Shari Johnson, more commonly known back then as the String Bean?

Such a discovery was bound to toss cold water on this whole seduction deal. Even though she hadn't laid eyes on Garrett in over a dozen years and had grown into a fairly attractive woman, it was highly unlikely that he could manage to throw old images aside and view her in the all-out sexy cast she desired.

And desire Garrett she did. Her childhood crush had expanded to wanton, womanly proportions. She measured every man she met by how Garrett had made her feel as a sensitive teenager. Ultimately she'd come to accept that it was not fair to the men she dated, not fair to herself. Once and for all she needed closure, and for closure she needed release.

The only truly satisfying release seemed to be in finally bedding the man. Living out every erotic fantasy she ever had about him and moving on.

Henceforth, the creation of Flame. Garrett would no doubt be smitten by her mystery and allure. Certainly enough to give in to her demands. Once sated, they both would go back to their separate worlds: he to his corporate kingdom of wealth and position, she to her humble coffee shop, the Beanery. Simple enough.

But oh so expensive! Shari half crumpled the receipt in her fingers. She hadn't expected to pay so much for this adventure. Big brother Dylan would have a fit if he ever found out where her half of Aunt Lucille's inheritance went.

She bit her artistically painted lip and stared down at the toes of her silver shoes. Dylan's fits were not to be taken lightly. A tremble of indecision coursed through her system. There was a choice to make: crack up and dash out, making apologies and a smaller donation to the literacy group tomorrow, or holding tight to the dream, taking on all the risks with a sizzling fear and anticipation.

In an unusual gesture of defiance, she stuffed the receipt and her woes into her evening bag for safekeeping. Garrett was worth the trouble, worth the risk.

"Here I am," he murmured into her hair moments later. "All yours."

Any lingering fears evaporated as she swiveled on her silver heels with an inward swoon, pretending to be startled by his presence. "So you are."

He raised his hands in the air. "Go ahead, have your way with me."

She couldn't have scripted his lines any better herself. Shari leisurely surveyed her forbidden fantasy. There was that old familiar teasing light in his eyes that was all the more adorable in adulthood. There was mature strength in those eyes now, as well, an intense and amorous glitter worthy of a full-grown man in command of a fortune and heaven only knew what else.

It had to be a dream....

"Do I know you?" he asked in the lapse of silence. "Somehow I think I should."

Damn, was she to be busted so soon? She fought the urge to stomp her foot on the plush carpet. He couldn't recognize her as the little mascot to the Brady High School basketball team, the playful pup, so invisible, inconsequential for so long. It would spoil everything, the glitter in his eyes would melt into something mushy and harmless. As predicted, she was liking Garrett intrigued and aroused a whole lot better.

She spoke from her diaphragm in a husky, exotic tone. "You can't know a thing about the Flame, I assure you."

"I know you're unlimited."

"You peeked." She coyly touched her hand to her heart, drawing attention to her plunging neckline, the plump creaminess of her breasts. "At my check."

"And a whole lot more." Garrett chuckled, taking the time to appreciate her loveliness in an up close and personal way: wide-set eyes, a startling aquamarine in color; high, striking cheekbones; full, kissable lips. Her

makeup was dramatic, more than he was used to. But
the overall result did her justice. She was exciting, tempting, a goddess. His voice dropped to a more serious note.
"What shall I call you? Really."

"Flame," she insisted.

"You can't be serious."

She ran a crimson fingernail along his jawline with a
stubborn look. "Now, who is supposed to be pleasing
whom here?"

Her touch was hot on his skin, living up to her name.
He quickly captured her hand, removing it from his
clean-shaven face, hovering closer. "C'mon now, fess
up."

She took her hand from his, her eyes narrowing.
"Meaning?"

"I mean," he whispered pointedly, "you seem to be
putting me on."

Her features smoothed. "Only in the nicest way, truly.
It's all a harmless game with absolutely no strings attached."

Silken strings were already tugging at Garrett, pulling
him under her spell. It wasn't like him to play along with
whimsy of any sort. As a rule he liked things clear,
aboveboard. But what red-blooded man could resist this
delightful paradox, an intriguing blend of candor and
mystery. "At least tell me your real name," he pressed.

She put her finger on his lips. "Stop thinking ordinary,
traditional. This is an adventure."

"But you know so much about me. From the auction
program, from the auctioneer."

"So make up for lost time. Give chase, examine me
thoroughly. Like this." She slid her gaze up and down
his body as she had during the bidding.

Garrett was astonished by her audacity. The whole
thing seemed so outrageous, naughty talk from a tempt-

ing stranger who had paid thousands of dollars for his company. He'd always considered himself a lucky man, but this setup took good fortune to new, impossible heights.

He cleared his throat, struggling with the passions threatening to surface below his belt. "We should be off."

She clutched his arm. "Yes, you have plans for me, don't you?"

Plans he desperately wished he could change. Garrett reached down to pick up the shimmery black shawl draped over her small suitcase and set it over her bare shoulders. He paused long enough to once again silently curse himself for planning this date around other people. But how could he have ever predicted such a delicious turn of events?

She laughed, twisting her face back to his. "You've spent half your time standing behind me."

Yes, half-afraid that she might hypnotize him into handing over his heart and soul. He gave her upper arms a squeeze, playing it sexy. "All the better to give chase, my dear." With a wink he picked up her case and ushered her toward the exit.

2

As Garrett's company limousine sped over the Bruckner Expressway on its way out of New York City, he made an effort to acquaint Flame with the other guests sharing the ride to Essex, Connecticut. Having her curvy body nestled beside him on the back seat would have been sheer ecstasy had they been alone. As it was, it was a sort of snaky hell that had kept him keeping his thigh to himself. She was within reach, but off-limits.

The two couples riding with them were handpicked conservatives meant to distract and entertain the cool socialite sort that Garrett had imagined as his date. The males, Herb Crater and Ronald Richtor, were his partners from the investment firm Crater, McNamara and Richtor; their respective spouses, Bernice and Nancy, were typical executive wives, heavily into charity work and furthering their husbands' careers. Older versions of what his mother, Gwen, wanted him to bring home.

Conversation was wary at first as the wives cautiously sized up Flame. She did well to put them at ease, confiding that she ran an import-export business in the city, and seemed well versed on a variety of subjects, everything from current affairs to the latest fashion. Garrett found himself proud of her for standing up to their interrogation, for coming off as sophisticated and wise beneath her sexy shell. Just as important, she appeared not the least bit interested in their husbands, who couldn't seem to take their eyes off her. This mildly shocked Garrett, as he had never seen his elder cohorts dazzled so by a woman. But Flame was indeed an exception to the rules, the maker of her own rules. How he looked forward to following some of them....

Garrett produced glass shakers of prepared martinis as they eased onto I-95 north. By the time they reached Route 9, leading directly into Essex, the car was nearly rocking with laughter and good cheer.

Essex, one of New England's oldest sailing communities, had always been a summer retreat for the Mc-Namaras. Shari vividly recalled that all through high school, Dylan and his basketball teammates mourned Garrett's departure from the city during the months of July and August. Now, staring out the window as the long vehicle rolled along Main Street, she recognized spots Garrett had long ago made come alive through imagery.

Amazingly, no one had particularly resented his wealth. He was singled out as a rich kid in their modest school, sure, one who attended Brady High because of its superb sports and mathematics programs. But from the start, he had a way of fitting in, being at ease, putting people at ease. A charm that Shari perceived as nothing less than magical.

Unbeknownst to her, Garrett was watching Flame stare dreamily out the car window. Did she have any clue to the ardent effect she was having on him? How unlike him it was to feel so anxious over a woman?

She turned then, meeting his gaze in the dim interior of the vehicle with a catlike glitter.

She knew all right. By God, it was all part of her game!

The limousine pulled into the pier shortly thereafter, parking in line with the other lavish automobiles belonging to Garrett's guests. They were greeted by a local boatman named Tom, who often ferried people out to their seaward crafts.

Tom tipped the skipper's hat he wore for the tourists. "Evening, Mr. McNamara. The *Temptation* set sail about twenty minutes ago. Your mother wasn't sure when you'd arrive and decided to go ahead."

Knowing looks were exchanged between the Richtors and the Craters. Garrett understood that along with many of Manhattan's social elite, they found Gwen McNamara deliberately difficult, a problem that had grown worse with the death of Garrett's father, Brent, some eighteen months earlier. If only his mom hadn't decided to play the grande dame tonight of all nights, with his precious Flame to entertain. But Gwen liked to pull rank just to keep the spotlight, and an apology seemed his only recourse.

"I hope you don't mind the inconvenience."

Nancy and Bernice favored him with understanding eyes, hastily covering for his errant parent.

"Nothing to it," Nancy gushed.

"Gwen was probably under some pressure by the guests to set sail," Bernice chimed in.

Herb and Ronald jovially backed them up.

Shari smiled benignly, thinking they were as clever actors as she. The Gwen McNamara she remembered couldn't be pressured by another living soul. She'd have King Kong in tears if he crossed her. There'd been countless instances during their teens when the matron had breezed into her family's coffee shop to make a power play and haul Garrett away from his friends on one pretext or another.

Garrett, too, knew the foursome was putting on a show, and he was almost grateful enough to hug each and every one of them. But it was Flame he chose to touch, with a gently massaging hand on her shawl-covered shoulder. "Okay by you, too?" he asked.

Shari winked. "Don't worry. I'm the flexible kind."

Tom was openly relieved by the group's sporting attitude. "I'm ready and willing to ferry you out then. Right this way." The couples paired off and followed the skipper, their dress shoes clattering on the wooden dock slats and echoing in the still night.

Tom hopped into a new fiberglass speedboat tethered to a pile, after taking their belongings aboard first. Garrett handed him Flame's case, then directed her gaze out to sea.

"Let me show you *Temptation* from a distance," he murmured close to her ear.

Ironically, he'd been showing her temptation from a distance for more years than she cared to remember. But in this case he was specifically referring to his family's yacht, so she dutifully stared out at the giant white craft bobbing out on the silvered Alantic waters, aglow with pinpoints of light.

"Isn't it a glorious picture?" he asked pensively.

"From stem to stern." She was secretly referring to his body, glorious front to back. His profile alone, cast to advantage in the soft romantic moonlight, was enough to make her knees go weak. It seemed incredible that he'd managed to reach the thirty mark a bachelor. She'd long awaited for news of his nuptials with equal measures of dread and hope, certain his marriage to someone else would finally free her from her sexual knot of frustration.

But time had reeled on, with Dylan seeing the very unattached Garrett live and up close at their ten-year high school reunion a couple of years ago. Still available, still gorgeous, still the kind of guy Dylan could easily connect with after years of separation.

Shari had wanted to think that fate had been saving him for her, but she knew better. Some happily-ever-after matches were strictly storybook. The most she could hope for was the night ahead of them, one powerful, memorable coupling to last a lifetime.

Garrett helped her aboard the speedboat, and with a soft rumble of the inboard motor, they began to glide through the bay. Nestled in Garrett's arms, she tried to keep her nerves in check. After all, maintaining an indifferent pose was crucial to the image she'd created, the core of her deception. Garrett had been given so many advantages at home that he'd been intensely attracted to the hard-to-get goals in school, everything from grades to girls to basketball plays. Shari was betting he hadn't outgrown that yearning. As successful as he'd become in his own right, she wagered the hunger for challenge had only intensified inside him.

The better the tease, the hotter his bother. The catchy phrase brought a naughty quirk to her lips.

Garrett pulled her closer on the seat, fervently wishing he could read her mind. Who was Flame in the everyday world? There were moments when she seemed in direct conflict with her snappy, invincible persona, like back on the docks when she stared needily upon him like the answer to some secret prayer. Was that merely part of her game or an unwitting revelation?

Garrett felt a fresh surge of pride as they approached the romantic *Temptation*. Music from the live band aboard, along with the sound of mingling voices, carried over the water in siren invitation.

To his delight, Flame was wearing traces of the same dewy expression she'd revealed on the docks. This was the ideal setting for amour, he knew. A place to peel away a lady's secrets, to gain some control, pull some strings of his own.

If only he hadn't flanked himself with all this unwanted, unnecessary company. But perhaps he could make it part of their game. It might be fun to let the sexual tension mount for hours, attempt to seduce her amid all his demanding guests.

The speedboat was anticipated and several of the *Temptation*'s efficient crew were standing by as the craft eased up to portside. Two uniformed stewards helped the guests aboard, ladies first. Shari, unaccustomed to navigating in her skintight beaded dress, stumbled a bit on the portable steps.

Once topside, Bernice and Nancy clucked over Flame like mother hens, edging so close that the folds of their full-length gowns formed a flag of white, red and gold in the gentle breeze.

Intent on having a taste of Flame before she was swallowed up into the throng, Garrett quickly boarded, wedging into the threesome to place an arm around her waist. Knowing the wives quite well, he was comfortable speaking plainly. "I was the one auctioned off, not you two."

Bernice regarded him in exasperation. "Oh, Garrett, she really should meet everyone in the main salon. They're all waiting—"

"I'm sure they're curious," he conceded. "But—"

"Of course they are," Nancy interrupted. "You shouldn't disappoint."

"There's time for everything, I'm sure," Shari huskily promised the ladies, while at the same time insinuating herself against Garrett to send him a clear message.

Garrett marveled at her cleverness, her ability to please them all at once. He was thrilled that she hadn't allowed the strong-willed matrons to carry her off at first try. She wanted to take their game to another level without delay. As it was, the minutes were ticking away at the speed of light. The adventure would be over all too soon if he didn't make the most of it. With a nod, he ushered her along the deck. "We'll catch up with you later."

"Okay," Herb called out jovially above the female murmurs of regret. "But Ron and I will be expecting a whirl on the dance floor."

Garrett paused to turn with a laugh. "Go ahead and boogie together all night long if you want. I don't mind if your wives don't."

Not waiting for a comeback, Garrett ushered Flame inside a dimly lit lounge. It seemed sealed off from the world, penetrated only by muted sounds of the distant merriment. He watched her turn slowly to take in the teak woodwork, the glass tables and yellow satin chairs with an expression that could have easily been misinterpreted as bedazzlement by some smitten idiot. But surely this kind of setup was routine to her, a rich and bold adventuress accustomed to having her way.

That's the image he felt best suited her. The image he intended to run with.

Shari laughed softly as her vivid aquamarine eyes rested upon him once more. "You know, I don't think those guys wanted to dance together at all."

He regarded her indulgently. "Naturally they wanted you. But I want you more, all for myself."

She tipped her chin just so for effect, causing her copper hair to shimmer in the glow of the lamp. "Hmm…I like the sound of that."

"If only it were so simple, the two of us agreeing. But I promised to deliver everybody a high-rolling bidder tonight. I can't conceal you much longer or they'll come looking. Old friends are like that."

Old friends. How old? Fleetingly, she wondered if it included anyone she knew from her family's coffee shop or from Brady High. Seemed unlikely. Besides, she was unrecognizable. If he hadn't a clue to her true identity, no one else from her past would, either.

"And there is my mother, Gwen," Garrett went on to say laboriously. "She's dying to meet you."

She would be, Shari thought flatly. Judging by her setting-sail stunt, it was likely Gwen was still desperately trying to control her only son at every turn.

"You have nothing to be concerned about," Garrett assured her, certain she'd stiffened a little in his arms. "It's only a formality."

Shari stared at the floor between their feet, keeping her voice airy. "I wonder if she'll think I'm your type."

"I'm afraid she's in the habit of digging me up well-educated hothouse flowers willing to be molded."

She cringed in a mildly mocking way. "I'm afraid I'm already molded."

"And quite nicely, too." Placing his hands on her hips, Garrett pulled her against him, making intimate body contact.

Her painted lips curved as she luxuriated in the gentle friction of his long, hard body against her soft curves. "Who knows, I just may go ahead and dazzle her."

"Dazzle me first."

Garrett dipped down in prelude to a kiss, staring into her face, cleverly painted like a china doll's. Persistent questions assailed him. Where did she come from? What was her story?

He had precious little time to wonder, however, as she took the initiative. Holding his jaw still, she slipped her tongue inside his mouth for sensitive exploration. He squeezed his eyes shut, allowing himself to let go completely with this uninhibited woman. All the while his hands roved the length of her gown, rippling over the layer of tiny red beads, crushing her closer.

Intent on not missing a thing, Shari kept her eyes wide

open. The fantasy was actually unfolding. The lover of her dreams was at this moment slowly giving way to his urges, thinking only of her, how to enjoy her and at the same time bring her satisfaction. Garrett, she knew, was one to always make sure his people were taken care of. Even as a kid, he was thoughtful that way.

He was bound to be a most generous lover…

Her body was quaking against his. Garrett could hardly believe it at first, but he pressed his hands into the small of her bare back to feel the vibration on his palms. His temples began to pound as he took over the kiss, bracing her firmly against him, driving his tongue into her mouth with more forceful strokes.

The kiss went on and on, carrying them higher into lusty territory near the point of no return.

She was playing another game, he realized, pushing him to the brink, daring him to take her now, when a cruiser of guests waited for him. It was with awesome willpower that Garrett finally took a deep, composing breath, releasing his lips from her soft, clingy ones, putting a smidgen of space between their bodies. "We'll…be missed."

"By anyone really important?"

He huffed, willing his pulse rate back to normalcy. "Well, yes. People from my turf, some very important to me."

She tugged at his dress tie, an odd light dancing in her aqua eyes. "But I own you for the night."

The blunt possessive claim swiftly brought his erection back to rock-hard attention. "You are my priority, honey. And later on, we're going to take the time to do this right."

The passion behind his promise and the intensity in his gray gaze caused a nervous quiver to race down Shari's spine. If only he knew he was in the process of making history in the small, ordinary life of Shari Johnson, bringing substance to her impossible infatuation. Such knowledge could do wild things to a man. In Garrett's case, she figured he'd either send her back on the first available skiff or bust his pants' zipper open with a lusty surge of ego.

In any case, she would proceed with the charade, take no chances on his response. She might have boarded the yacht a young woman of limited sexual experience, but she certainly wasn't going to leave in the same condition!

CINDERELLA AT THE BALL. That's how Shari felt as she stepped into the yacht's main salon on Garrett's arm. The decor was lavish with teak trim and flooring, a circular black-lacquered bar, U-shaped settees and a huge buffet table full of tempting dishes. The atmosphere was electric with high society guests mingling, dancing to the easy-listening music of a quartet.

Garrett shared her excitement for reasons of his own. This sort of bash was routine to him, but having such a striking, vivacious partner at his side shook things up dramatically. People were staring, admiring, guessing. He wanted to flaunt her and yet keep her all to himself. Dancing seemed the best way to accomplish that, so Garrett led her out onto the polished floor for some slow but showy maneuvers.

As poor luck would have it, the band suddenly announced a set of livelier numbers then, shifting from easy-rhythm elevator music to a Latin number that would require a lot more dance skill.

Garrett gazed down at her hesitantly. "Do you mambo?"

"Yes," she quipped, listening to the tune. "And I love the 'Mambo Jambo.'"

She even knew the song. Impressed, Garrett eagerly

took her in his arms and led her forward in quick and flashy movement. It was as though they were of one mind, stepping and turning in graceful unison. He dared himself to wonder if it was an omen, if this fit was perfect, meant to last.

Common sense suggested that Garrett hardly knew Flame well enough to dream so big. And he wasn't the type who bought into love at first sight. Still, they seemed to share an underlying chemistry, as with very old acquaintances who clicked after months apart.

With any luck, this feeling could help cut through the customary red tape involved in first dates, perhaps lead right into bed.

Garrett couldn't stop thinking of sex as he held Flame in his arms, inhaling her heavy provocative scent, staring into her sparkling aqua eyes. She was made for love-making with her slender curves and strong limbs. He couldn't help imagining all the wonderful positions...

The band eased right into a cha-cha number, 'Peanut Vendor'. Amazingly, Flame followed him into it without a word. Garrett guided her in the rote forward-backward quickstep motion, reveling in the way her body moved with his, so effortlessly, so erotically. He'd never understood before the true meaning of the mating dance....

Garrett wanted her desperately! Shari read a powerful yearning in his face as he clung to her, dominating their moves, testing her with more forceful commands. He had to be marveling over the perfect fit between them, her ability to flow flawlessly across the floor in his arms. Simply explained, since they'd shared a dance teacher some years ago.

Images of his senior prom flashed before her eyes. He'd looked particularly dashing in his tuxedo, and extremely remote as he gazed right through her like a windowpane, no doubt calculating how he could charm his date-of-the-moment. How hurt she'd been that he'd been too distracted to see her on that special night. She'd been too young to date him, but any small recognition would've soothed the disappointment.

He'd always dated like an anxious wanderer, looking for the perfect match. Rumor said he still had the same method of operation. All in all, it fit into her fantasy perfectly. They would share the ultimate pleasures, then part before reality could crash through and make it all seem ordinary. Then Garrett would spend the next decade thinking about her, rather than vice versa. Certainly a just turnabout.

They were into their third dance when the first intruder cut in on Garrett's action. Unfortunately, it wasn't a male he could brush off but Nancy, Ronald Richtor's wife. She was tapping on Flame's shoulder with determination. With a swirl of bodies and Nancy's golden hemline, she and Garrett were off, bouncing to the foxtrot.

Shari didn't mind the break. She immediately headed for the circular bar and ordered a daiquiri. Just as she was easing up on one of the cushioned stools, Gwen McNamara appeared at her side, introducing herself in a gush.

"M'dear, Nancy and Bernice have told me all about you."

"Have they really?" Shari nodded at the bartender as he set a stemmed glass before her. She took a sip of her tangy citrus drink, hoping to disguise her smirk. "How kind." How convenient. How amusing. Getting unexpected help in spreading her tale.

"I mean," Gwen restated, "they've told me what they know."

Which unfortunately wouldn't be enough for the controlling Gwen. Not caring to be interrogated, Shari swiftly turned the tables to Gwen's favorite subject: herself. "My reputation can't hold a candle to yours, Mrs. McNamara," she said sweetly. "You are a legend in Manhattan, chairing committees in some of the finest organizations, hosting lavish events for the arts."

"Do call me Gwen, please." She leaned closer to Shari's stool, as though intent on sharing a girlish confidence. Gwen couldn't quite pull it off, however, looking a bit too cronelike to elicit trust. It was difficult to define the flaw, as Gwen was battling the ravages of time with understated elegance, her hair styled in a subtle silver bob, her face- and breast-lifts more of a freshener than a cheerleader makeover.

Admittedly, a fine picture on the surface. Still, Shari felt no girlish ease here. An all-too-familiar severity centered around Gwen's eyes and mouth, a timeless grimness that defined her as one who could chew up nails like pretzel sticks.

"Surely you can tell me your true story," Gwen coaxed. "Is Flame a stage name? I am quite the devoted theater buff but can't say I've ever heard of you."

"I don't know the first thing about acting," she replied innocuously.

"Oh, come now—" Gwen broke off, frowning at Shari's professional makeup job.

Shari raised her glass to her flawless mask, as though fearing the older woman could tear it off somehow. "This masquerade is all in the spirit of fun, believe me. Charity functions can prove tedious at times and meeting strangers can be awkward. I decided to appear the enigma, thinking it might lighten the circumstances."

Gwen gave the matter consideration while waiting for a martini. When she turned back to Shari, drink in hand, she was beaming with approval. "I try to give credit where it is due, and I must say you deserve it here. Party-goers will be talking about you in the days to come and that will surely lead to more contributions to literacy. As for Garrett's state, whatever you've done so far has pleased him immensely."

"All we've shared is small talk," Shari demurred.

Gwen tasted her drink with an ambitious glint in her eye. "Perhaps the two of you share more interests than you know. New relationships are so exciting, the un-knowns, the challenges. And this new spin of yours..." Gwen looked ready for a fresh round of interrogation, then bit her lip and patted the young woman's hand on the bar. "Never mind, I played my own games when I was your age. You are absolutely charming. I say rattle Garrett if you can. He works far too hard and can use the playtime."

Shari stared off in wonderment. An unexpected bo-nus: Gwen actually liked her. Or rather, Gwen liked the sophisticated monied person she appeared to be. Mrs. McNamara would blow a fuse if confronted with the truth, that the goddess behind the greasepaint was al-most as poor as the fabled Cinderella and all she could hope to share with her son was one slow burn between the sheets.

Garrett hoped to reclaim Flame after his dance with Nancy, but it was not to be. All his female guests ex-pected a whirl on the dance floor, as was customary, and he had no choice but to oblige. This was especially tough when he watched his mother move in on his date at the bar across the salon. As was customary, Gwen was rid-ing high as the grande dame who called the shots.

Suddenly it occurred to him that Gwen might have gone further than recommending him for the auction, that she might have actually set Flame up as top bidder in hopes of a love match.

His heart sank over the prospect. What if Flame was one of *them:* a prospective daughter-in-law handpicked by Gwen, part of her finicky crowd, full of preconceived notions about what a relationship should entail, meek and unresponsive in bed.

Garrett was bored with such women and Gwen knew it. So presumably, if she were to try again, she'd need an entirely different approach. He could almost hear her instructions: "Entice the boy in a whole new way, prove irresistible, unattainable, even mystic—he'll fall like a rock."

If it proved to be true, this was her finest effort, a whole new level of entrapment. The very idea was harshly claustrophobic. Suddenly he needed some air. Badly.

The deck was where Shari ultimately discovered him, leaning against the guardrail, staring grimly out to sea.

"Shame on you, escaping your own party."

He scowled. "Suddenly I couldn't breathe."

She recognized that scowl for all it was worth. The tightness of jaw, the furrow of brow signaled real anger. Had he figured things out? Did the very idea insult him to this degree? "Speak, man," she wheedled cheerfully.

"I saw you speaking to my mother at the bar," he said flatly.

Her pulse tripped as she tried to second-guess him. Was Gwen's cheer phony? Had Gwen gotten to him, suggested she wasn't their kind? The inescapable feeling that she wasn't good enough to be here, aboard this boat, mingling with these powerful people, reared its ugly head and took some of the starch out of her spine. "What did your mother say, Garrett?"

"That's my question to you."

"Nothing much. She seemed to like me."

"Did she?"

She caught her breath as he gripped her bare upper arms. "What's the matter?"

He searched her face. "I hoped I could tell, but I can't."

"What!"

His voice could have ground coffee beans. "If you're one of hers."

"Excuse me?"

"Another eligible bride tossed at me like a rag doll."

"That's what you think!"

"A Gwen McNamara creation," he raved on. "A real live phony."

Shari was torn between sympathy and irritation. It was clear back at the bar that Gwen still liked to play a heavy hand in her son's life. But how dare he suggest collusion without proof? "I have absolutely no connection to Gwen," she scolded. "Your mother was polite, that's all. If you don't believe me, Garrett, this was a mistake, a waste—"

Her righteous indignation was all too real. Afraid he might end up spoiling things, Garrett put a finger to her mouth, gathering her close. "Okay, seems I've jumped the gun."

She nipped the finger at her lips. "You did."

"Sorry I jumped to conclusions. But with Mother, I often expect the worst and get it."

"I understand," she said softly.

Garrett was somewhat bewildered by the sincerity in her claim but couldn't help feeding off her support. How could he have ever mistaken Flame for one of his mother's prospects, the kind who gushed over Gwen or simpered at her heels. "It's just that you've been so wonderful," he sought to explain, pulling her even closer. "The very idea that you might not be what you seem upset me."

Shari burrowed her face against his shirt, shaken by

their exchange. This was supposed to be a lark, every single minute of it. Now here they were, getting emotional, personal and supportive—all with their clothes on. This was supposed to be about lust and chicanery and bare skin! Still, she allowed precious, expensive auctioned-off minutes to pass as they shared a sense of quiet togetherness.

He finally crooked a finger under her chin and lifted her face to his. "So, you ready to toss me overboard for spoiling your game plan?"

She swallowed hard, finding her throat was almost closed. "Nothing's spoiled. I wanted this evening with you more than anything, Garrett, and we still have that. It's between the two of us, no one else."

Garrett loosened in relief. He was back in business, the dream was drifting back in place. Longing to possess her all over again, he captured her mouth with his, kissing her deeply, charging himself on her energy cache. When he came up for air, his voice was hoarse. "You are the real thing, aren't you?"

She took his hand and placed it beneath the strap of her gown above her heart. "I am this real."

He closed his eyes, using his palm to absorb the heat of her skin, the beat of her heart. "Very real." His hand slipped lower, into the halter of her gown, grazing her nipple. She sighed softly, wantonly, initiating another kiss. He crowded her against the rail, rolling her nipple between his thumb and finger until it hardened. They shared a quiet groan of pleasure.

"Oh, here you are!"

They were jarred by Herb Crater as he emerged from the shadows, his white dinner jacket a stark standout. He strolled closer, puffing on a cigar. Twisting his squat body, he called out, "Here they are, Ron!"

Ronald Richtor emerged from the same general area.

He tipped his burning cigar at them. "Hope you don't mind, Garrett. We raided your stash of Cubans in the study."

"You're always welcome," Garrett said briskly, using his body as a shield as he removed his hand from Flame's dress.

As predicted, his partners were after her, intent upon bringing her back to the salon for some serious partying. It was to be expected, of course, playing out exactly as he'd arranged it. To think he'd deliberately surrounded them with people. He kept his smile steady. They had the whole night.

3

"LOOKING AT YOUR WATCH AGAIN, Garrett? You've been doing that ever since we moored half an hour ago."

"Oh, Mother." Garrett smiled thinly, annoyed that she'd caught him counting down the party's end like a randy teenager. "I was seeing guests go down the gangway and figuring when they could hope to arrive back in Manhattan. Before dawn, I'd say."

"I'll accept that excuse." Gwen gazed around the salon. "Where's Flame, by the way?"

"Freshening up is the official story. But after the way she was handed off from one dancer to the next, I imagine she's really hiding out."

"I saw you cutting in regularly enough."

"Yes, and every time she complained of pinched toes and demanded her money back. Must say I understood, as my own feet are beginning to hurt. Everyone wants a whirl with the host at these things."

"Well, I'm hoping you have one last dance in you." She gestured to the near-empty dance floor.

Garrett knew what she wanted, a chance to trap him for some interrogation concerning Flame. "Mother," he said with strained politeness, "I should be on the docks."

She tugged at his elbow with a pouty look. "The crew can manage for a few minutes. And you've made your goodbye speech at the mike. Come on, you've been neglecting me all night long."

Garrett took his petite mother in his arms and they

swayed to the tune of some soft jazz. He would have preferred something louder, making conversation an impossibility, but no such luck.

"She's lovely, darling," Gwen remarked at length.

Garrett remained sober. "Yes, the *Temptation* is a worthy craft."

"I mean Flame and you know it."

"Hmm..." He glided and twirled them round the floor, looking off into space.

"You aren't annoyed that it was I who got you involved in the auction in the first place, are you?"

His tensing gaze landed back on her. "I did originally have some unkind visions of auctioning you off as first prize at an aluminum siding convention—"

"You devil!"

"But the feeling passed once I met the top bidder."

Gwen grinned craftily. "I suppose you thought I was responsible for her, as well."

He wouldn't allow her the satisfaction of knowing he had feared as much. "No chance," he scoffed. "She easily surpasses your best efforts."

Gwen struggled not to take offense. "Very true. I must confess I do wish I could take credit for her."

"Really? So soon?" he mocked in wonder. "It's not like you to approve of a stranger without deep scrutiny, the old acid test."

She was matter-of-fact. "Be assured I did dig deep. We had a late snack at the buffet and a sit-down chat. Her etiquette proved impeccable, her diction remarkable, her knowledge of the arts thorough."

"Good signs," Garrett agreed, looking a bit hesitant. "She didn't overindulge on anything, did she?"

"Not to worry, she drank and ate in moderation." She paused as Garrett's smirk deepened. "You're teasing."

"Possibly."

Gwen frowned. "Joke all you want, but it's a serious matter—to know that she's unlikely to get puffy and flabby over time."

"I've only known this woman for several hours. It's ridiculous to push so hard."

"But you are thirty, Garrett. The passage of time is fast becoming an issue if you hope to start a family."

Gwen delivered the message with rapid gunfire accuracy. How he hated it when she managed to pop up with the occasional nugget of wisdom. He did want to settle down with the right woman—he just wanted to handle the required search himself.

"That isn't all I discovered," Gwen went on to confide. "She knows all the hits currently on Broadway, her share of actors—"

"I don't give a damn about that!"

"Surely it should count for something in the grand scheme."

"But does she know her way around Wall Street," Garrett demanded, "her share of brokers?"

She rolled her eyes. "And that is exclusively your turf."

Garrett gave her a final twirl as the music died away. "It's all my turf, Mother. My choice to decide what really matters most in the long run."

She stomped her satin shoe beneath the sweeping hem of her gown. "Even when I approve, you're angry."

"I'm not angry," he said mildly, "just vaguely annoyed and tired of playing host."

"Understandable. I just want to make sure you appreciate this opportunity. And to show you the extent of my good faith, I am leaving with the guests."

He stumbled back, his surprise mocking. "You're not!"

She beamed grandly. "I am. I'm riding back to the city with the Richtors just to give you some space."

Garrett kissed Gwen's silvered bangs. "Thanks."

"All I ask is that you find out who she really is." Her thin brows narrowed. "That should be your most important goal."

The party was officially over then. The band made tracks to the buffet table to help themselves before the catering staff could clear everything away. Most of the guests had departed, but the Richtors were lingering in the salon, enjoying a final drink while they waited for Gwen. Garrett and his mother joined them. The women exchanged pleasantries about the evening while Garrett and Ronald briefly conferred on a business matter to be further addressed Monday morning.

That was when Garrett caught a whiff of a familiar perfume. Suffused with pleasure, he turned to find Flame standing behind him in her crimson dress. She eased into the gathering, elegant and striking despite the wee hour.

"Safe to come out now?" she piped up.

"Very," Ronald assured jovially. "The music's died and all the toe stompers have bailed."

"Even Mother's leaving," Garrett reported with pleasure.

Gwen McNamara, the biggest toe stomper of them all in Shari's mind. Ever watchful of her manners, though, she turned to the matriarch with a token protest. "You're not going because of me, I hope."

"In a way, yes," Gwen admitted. "You made a most generous bid for this evening with my son and it is yours by all rights."

Garrett beamed proudly. "Well put, Mother. As I see it, the sooner you all leave, the sooner I'll start to miss you."

Gwen's lips thinned. "Damn liar."

The accusation brought a round of hearty laughter from the group, which Garrett skillfully moved topside and down the gangway in record time. With a wave and final farewell, he returned to the breezy deck to stand beside Flame, who was lost in thought, rubbing her bare arms for warmth.

"You're chilly." He stripped off his jacket and wrapped it around her. "We should probably go inside."

She took his wrist firmly and turned it over to check his watch. "I can't believe it's past one."

And he couldn't believe any of this was happening. "Tell me what you want," he coaxed huskily. "This is your show, your night."

"I would like my overnight case first, I suppose. Do you know where it is?"

"In my quarters," he admitted, rubbing his mouth to cover a nervous twitch. Had he been presumptuous sending it there? The brisk night air was beginning to clear his head, making him wonder if she was more tease than substance. Perhaps she'd been caught up in the moment earlier on when they'd kissed in the stateroom. Perhaps now that they were truly alone, things would be different. "I can have the case moved to any number of places," he rushed to assure her. "You're welcome to choose."

Her lips curved in sensual invitation, reaffirming her intentions. "I would like to see yours for a start."

"My what?"

"Your everything."

He put an arm around her shoulders and led her down the deck. "I'm sold. All over again."

"SO THIS IS YOUR BEDROOM." She entered his quarters with a rustle of beaded gown, pausing to slip off her sandals and hook them on her fingers by the straps.

"Actually, it's the grand master suite," he corrected gently. "Luxury tugs this size have fancy names for things. You should understand, with your fancy name."

Shari tried to keep her composure as she toured the spacious room, but it was difficult not to be dazzled like a child in a candy store. Everything gleamed, from the paneled walls and ceiling to the glowing wall sconces and heavy furniture. The king-size bed was the crowning centerpiece, boxed in teak, its cream-colored spread turned down to reveal pristine white sheets and pillows.

She didn't realize Garrett had moved into the master bath until the light switched on. "Come in here, Flame."

Her pseudonym sounded so appealing in his care, a symbol of how Garrett treated her in general. He was gentle, teasing, the full-grown male she imagined him to be. She floated across the carpet in bare feet, wondering if he had any idea how desperately she wanted to make passionate love to him.

Garrett in his tuxedo. Try as she might, she couldn't erase the memory of him at the age of eighteen, dressed in similar fashion for his senior prom. She'd lain awake for hours that night, waiting for her brother, Dylan, to return with news of the event, some hint of how much fun Garrett had had. Fourteen at the time, she'd been charged with an innocent sexual frustration, tortured over whether Garrett was making love to his date, a nameless debutante chosen by Gwen. Shari never found out any of the important details. Dylan came home at a decent hour, but only because he'd broken up with his girlfriend, Allison Walker. He didn't know or care what Garrett's itinerary was.

Amazing, she remembered that night far more clearly than she did her own senior prom.

"Here's your case." Garrett was standing by the marble sink, holding her overnight bag. Reliving prom night always left her feeling like the String Bean again, a gangly kid sister to Garrett, Dylan and many others. Shari couldn't help glancing in one of the mirrors to make sure her makeup and hair were in place. She looked fine, still the sizzling seductress. It gave her the confidence to speak plainly, to follow through.

"Put that down, Garrett."

The husky command startled him. "But I thought you wanted it."

Her aqua gaze gleamed. "I'll show you what I want."

Garrett turned to set the case back on the sink, electric with expectation. This game just kept getting better. Every phase held wonder, tension. His heart nearly stopped as she advanced on him with purpose. Before he could make any kind of overture, she was pinning him against the vanity with her slender body, working loose the knot of his tie.

Women never played the aggressor with him in the bedroom, presumably because of his high-powered position in professional and social circles. How often he'd wondered what such a come-on would be like. And now it was happening. This mysterious enchantress sought him out with gusto and was proceeding to have her way with him.

His blood began to bubble with heat. Grabbing her hair, Garrett sought her mouth, kissing her hungrily, dazedly. It was all too sweet, too delicious, too outrageous.

She was breathless when she tore her mouth free. "I hope I'm not pushing you."

He grinned wickedly. "Like a little steam engine."

"I can stop…"

He placed her hand over his solid sex. "Not anymore. I couldn't bear it."

Encouraged, she continued to loosen his clothing, stripping away his shirt, his shoes, socks, trousers. Left in only his briefs, he stilled her hands. "When are you taking something off?"

"Now if you like." She straightened, reached beneath her fall of copper hair to the nape of her neck to unhook her heavy beaded dress. It fell to the marble floor in a red, glistening heap. "Satisfied?"

More like mesmerized. Garrett blinked in disbelief. She was standing before him completely nude. Lovely, shapely, calmly. High plump breasts, gently curving hips. It was a struggle to find his voice. "All night long...you were...like that...under there!"

She raised a slender thigh in a coquettish pose. "Wonder which of your friends would've guessed they were dancing the night away with a woman wearing no underwear."

"Mmm... I'm sure some of them were pretending as much on their own."

"Ah, you think so." She feigned surprise, easing back between his parted legs. "Well, even so, I was all yours all the time."

He groaned softly as her long red fingernails began to skim his solid, hair-dusted thighs, scrape the leg openings of his briefs. He instinctively leaned back slightly on the marble surface as her fingers crawled higher to his waistband. Despite his determination to remain as cool as she was, he couldn't help growling like a bear when she dipped inside his briefs to clench his rigid flesh.

Space and time were lost to him as she massaged his intimate places. Eventually he could no longer stand the restraint and began to tug his briefs free of his hips. With a throaty chuckle, Flame took over, pulling them free with her toes. He took the moment to produce a condom from a vanity drawer, which she very erotically put in place.

Wanting to return all the attention, Garrett swiftly took the initiative. Anxious to feel her silken skin against his, he angled her along his half-lounging form.

Burrowing in, Shari rested her cheek on his broad chest. "Touch me."

Large, strong hands stroked her back, her bottom, kneading her flesh, making her shudder. She didn't recognize her own purring sounds, nor could she ever recall such a heightened arousal.

"Is this the way you like it, honey?"

"Hmm…"

With answering moans he kissed her hair and nibbled her ear. "Want to get wet?"

"We are."

"I mean in the whirlpool bathtub, right behind you."

She'd noticed the giant marble tub, of course. But she didn't dare go near it with her disguise. For the first time all evening, she visibly faltered. "Not tonight."

"Oh, c'mon, it'll be fun."

She shook her head against his chest.

He squeezed her torso harder, gently lifting her over his groin with a tantalizing rub. "What's the matter, afraid you'll melt?"

Yes! As crazy as it sounded, he'd hit upon the truth.

"Hard as I try," he said stubbornly, "I can't quite get the image of us in there out of my mind."

Then she would have to erase it for him, Shari thought. And there was only one sure way. As he drew her up over his body again, she braced her hands on his shoulders, curled her legs around his waist and took his erection inside her.

He gasped in shock as ripples of pleasure coursed his system. "Oh, baby…"

She tipped her head back with a secret triumphant smile as he clamped steadying hands to her waist. There were no more protests as he took a nipple into his mouth for a slow, arousing suckle, no more suggestions as he pumped her with a steady, friction-causing rhythm.

Flame could be the ultimate distraction when necessary. Her powers were awesome, heady, unlimited.

They climaxed quickly. No surprise, as their foreplay had been going on for hours, since the moment Garrett spotted her beyond the footlights at the Waldorf.

"Sure you don't want to take a dip in the tub?" he asked again, removing the condom and tossing it in a wastebasket.

He was so persistent about that dip! Thinking fast, Shari stood on tiptoe and gave him a long, lingering kiss. Before long, he began to swell all over again.

Garrett was willing to give up on the tub to please her, but he did want to take their passion to a more comfortable surface just the same. He abruptly scooped her up against his chest, his gray eyes gleaming with rekindled lust. "Any objections to bed?"

"Hold on. You're forgetting something."

He froze in panic, staring down at her supple body draped over his strong arms. "Like what?"

"These." She wiggled a little in his grasp, reaching into the vanity drawer for the box full of condoms.

"Oh, those!"

"What else could I possibly need right now?"

He carried her into the adjoining room, releasing a low whistle of relief. "For a minute there, I thought maybe you wanted some flowery assurances. Which, I can tell you, I flub up miserably."

"Not Flame," she assured him, clinging to his neck.

"She finds such things totally unnecessary." Dull Shari might expect something like that, but he wouldn't have given Shari a second glance in the first place, so it didn't matter. This was the kind of woman Garrett would go for without deliberation: flashy, careless, presenting a challenge.

Garrett gently tossed her on the open bed, then followed her down to the white sheets. The bedding was soft to the skin. Shari could only imagine the standards of upkeep the McNamaras insisted upon in all their residences. It was in such stark contrast to the modest building in Manhattan that held the Beanery and its upstairs living quarters occupied by Dylan and her.

Garrett was bearing down on her now, closing his mouth over one nipple, then the other. Slowly he began to kiss the length of her belly, tease the concave surface of her navel. With painstaking attention he blazed a trail of fire with his mouth, until she began to writhe and whimper.

This couldn't be happening. Not with her dream man.

And it was only getting hotter. She was trembling by the time he parted her legs, raised her knees. Still he was leisurely, searing the tender skin of her thighs with wet kisses. Low, masculine groans of hunger unfamiliar to her filled the room as he stroked her sex with his tongue, nibbling on sensitive skin no man had ever probed so intimately.

If he ever found out who she was...

But he wouldn't find out. Shari squeezed her eyes shut, putting a deliberate shutter over the past. Enjoying this once-in-a-lifetime encounter was all that mattered.

Garrett was in a timeless bubble as he explored her body, tasting, tickling, caressing. She was up for anything, he discovered. Hours drifted by as they tried many positions, looking for fresh sensations. He couldn't get enough of her, or she of him. How tempted he'd been to demand her true identity, insist she come clean so they could plan future contact. But he sensed it would spoil it for her. She obviously relished her secrets. Considering his lavish price tag, what could he do but give in to her wishes? All her wishes....

It was in complete exhaustion that they finally drifted off to sleep in the giant, rumpled bed. Garrett's last thought was that he'd confront her in the morning once their time together was off the bachelor-auction meter. He'd make her talk somehow.

SUNLIGHT WAS SPILLING through the portholes when Garrett stirred the following day. With eyes closed, he took a few minutes to review the night, convince himself that it truly happened, that dreams did indeed come true. He stretched and called for Flame, hoping she'd crawl into his arms. When she didn't respond he began to pat the bed. When he found it empty, his eyes flew open in a panic. She was nowhere in sight and the digital clock on the nightstand read 7:48. He never slept this late!

With panther movements, he lunged out of bed and tore into the bathroom. He nearly bounced off the walls as he took in details. There was not a trace of her any-place.

Perhaps it had all been a dream. The very best dream a guy could ever hope to have, with a vivid plot to en-hance the all-consuming sex scenes.

Shaking his head, he wandered back to the bed. Hands on hips, he surveyed the area, spotting discarded evi-dence of their passion in the wastebasket beneath the nightstand. A tight smirk played across his face. It hap-pened, all right. The Flame was real and hot enough to leave a permanent brand on him.

He clenched his fists at his sides. How could she do this, make that lavish bid for him, share his bed, then disappear without bringing closure to the game by revealing herself?

Fuming over her sneakiness and his own shortsightedness, he stomped over to a cabinet for a pair of briefs. Yanking them on, he found himself wondering about her position on the panty issue. Did she ever wear them?

He threw his hands up in despair. How could he possibly hope to live in peace until he discovered whether she ever wore panties? Or liked his favorite foods? Or slept late on weekends? Or had a decent portfolio for her assets?

Reaching into a locker, he grabbed some jeans and a sweatshirt. Then he pressed a button on the wall intercom to reach one of the crew.

"Yessir, this is Clyde."

Garrett smiled; he especially liked this first mate. He'd been with the family for years. "I'm wondering, Clyde, if you know what happened to the lady I had aboard earlier on…"

"Oh, yes. She left in the catering truck some time ago. Probably back in Manhattan by now."

"Okay. Thanks." He took his finger off the button. Dammit! Gone without a trace.

Or was she? Out of the corner of his eye he spotted something unusual on the pale carpet, glistening in a shaft of sunlight. A key ring. He quickly scooped it up and turned it over in his hand. A green plastic disk holding a single key on a metal loop. He'd seen the kind all over town, produced in mass quantity, with a personalized advertisement for a particular service or establishment.

This one was for a place called the Beanery. The plastic disk was scuffed and speckled with pink nail polish, but the name jumped out at him with clarity, bringing on a flood of pleasant memories. His old high school hangout on West Forty-fifth and Eighth. He hadn't been there in years. What could a goddess like Flame possibly have to do with a modest coffee shop like the Johnsons'? It had to be her key ring, didn't it? Surely no one else had been in his suite. Still, what were the odds? The crazy, impossible odds?

He squeezed the plastic disk, deciding it was a talisman. Because of this connection to his past, he would have a chance of finding his future.

Suddenly it occurred to him that perhaps she'd left it on purpose, as a clue to her identity. Was she aware he already knew the place, or was that simply a crazy coincidence? The possibilities tumbled through his mind, energizing him, frustrating him.

His main focus should be the fact that she probably wanted him to give chase, probably wanted to be found. Discovering her in her real world would bring their game to a higher level. Then they could go on, higher and higher still.

For the first time in his life, Garrett McNamara was very sure he'd met the woman of his dreams, the woman he might well come to call his wife.

TRACY WEBSTER WASN'T accustomed to people pounding on her apartment door before 8:00 a.m. on a Sunday. Whoever it was had better be prepared for some heat.

A quick check through the peephole quickly lightened her mood. In a way, her visitor was the heat. She quickly tripped the locks and opened the door wide. "What on earth are you doing here, *Flame*?"

Shari barged inside the tiny studio space in a cloud of exasperation and euphoria, nearly mowing Tracy down with her boxy overnight case. "You know better than to call me that, Trace. It's well past sunup and, as planned, the dream date is over."

Tracy closed the door and shrewdly eyed her best pal. "Well, if you're going to crash here, Miss Shari Johnson, you're going to give me a full and uncensored report. You can start with the reason why you're in Greenwich Village when you have a perfectly fine apartment above the Beanery? Which is set to open in a couple of hours, in case you've forgotten."

"I know we're due at work." Shari padded into Tracy's bathroom and got the shower running. She stripped off the heavy beaded gown in a fit of self-recrimination. "But damned if I didn't lose my key someplace. Naturally I couldn't hope to get by that tyrant I call a brother without one. Any noise in the hallway and Dylan would be out his door full of questions and accusations." She touched her coppery hair and rouged cheek. "I couldn't let him see me like this."

"No, not after all the trouble we went to to keep this adventure of yours a secret." Tracy clutched the lapels of her white terry robe, sizing her friend up like a litigator. "So the dream is over.... Tell me, dare we place it in the consummate dream category?"

Shari stepped into the tub enclosure, rummaging through Tracy's plastic basket of toiletries on a shelf under the nozzle. "We certainly may," she reported smugly before drawing the plastic shower curtain closed.

Tracy's scream bounced off the tiled walls. "You actually did it—with Garrett McNamara!"

Shari peeped out, brimming with glee. "Yup."

"And it was..."

"Everything I hoped it would be," she shouted above the jet spray.

A little spurting water didn't stop Tracy from peering

inside the tub. "Did he know you? Did he guess any of it?"

Shari unscrewed the top from a bottle of shampoo, awestruck. "He was clueless through the whole night."

"But captivated?"

"Totally."

They shared delighted laughter.

"So, he teach you any new tricks?"

Shari scrubbed her hair and skin with liquid soap, the water sluicing down her body and turning a rainbow of earth tones. "Most of it was new to me. The few guys I've had sex with were into very ordinary methods."

"But that's partly your own fault," Tracy reasoned. "Any man who's even half-polite would realize you weren't open to the extras."

"True. I've never given any man much encouragement. But I do know how to, it seems. Garrett didn't miss any of my signals."

"You left Magda's house a flashing neon sign of sexuality! Naturally Garrett found you obliging."

Shari made a sour face. "It's a sign that won't be posted for the general public ever. Though I wonder if a person shows any obvious signs of change after a night of multiple orgasms."

"Probably only if you walk funny." Tracy doubled over with laughter.

Shari sighed dreamily, ignoring her pal's earthy retort. "It was so hard to leave him, Trace, sound asleep in bed on his luxury yacht. The slightest nudge and I know he would've been good for another heavenly roll in the sheets."

"Luxury yacht, instant arousal." Tracy shook her head with force, silken black hair swirling round her elbows. "I gotta get out of that coffee shop of yours more often!"

Shari sighed, philosophical. "Don't forget it was a

once-in-a-lifetime fantasy night, a Cinderella adventure without the fairy-tale happy ending. I went into it knowing a tycoon like Garrett could never take a working girl like me seriously in the light of day."

"S'pose not. But maybe if he came to realize who he was playing around with—"

"It would only make matters worse!" Shari squealed at the very idea, shutting off the faucet. "The last thing Garrett would like to hear is that he'd just seduced his high school pal's little sister—*the String Bean.*"

Tracy tossed her a towel. "C'mon, you'd never be mistaken for a string bean now."

"You don't understand," Shari insisted, briskly drying her skin. "It was more than an aside reference. I wasn't a string bean. I was *the* String Bean, the skinny, goofy mascot of the Beanery. Get the play on words? A bean at the Beanery?"

"That's stupid."

"Most high school jocks can be at times. It was just one of those awkward situations that has no end, no cure. Brady High's basketball team regarded me as a mere child the whole time they used our place as their hangout. There were four full years between us and I never made it to Brady High during their reign."

Tracy peeled down to her red nightshirt, giving Shari her robe. "It does add up, I suppose. Dylan still treats you like a child sometimes, even though the two of you now share joint ownership of the Beanery."

Shari donned the terry wrap with a grimace, looping a towel around her dripping head. "Yes. Bless my folks for realizing that they couldn't retire to Florida without an even split of the shop." She turned to her case on the sink to dig for her toothbrush. "So, have you eaten yet?"

"You telling me you're hungry?"

Shari beamed. "Ravenous."

"As it happens, I'm just fixing some French toast."

"Hmm…my favorite."

Tracy backed out of the room, pausing in the doorway to wag a finger. "Just be prepared to sing for your breakfast."

Shari entered the kitchen shortly thereafter, still wrapped in terry cloth from head to ankles. Tracy had a grip on a black frying pan and was shoveling some bubbly wedges of toast onto plates at the table. She paused to inspect the friend she knew and loved, who was now back to her softer, gentler self. "Gee, those green contacts really did jazz up your eyes, didn't they?"

Shari sank in a chair with a flutter of lashes. "Yup. But it's back to these old baby blues for good. After we eat I'll have to hunt up my specs. They're hidden in the bottom of my overnight case."

Tracy shoved the pan back on the stove then returned to take a seat. "Orange juice?"

"Yeah. I'll pour." Shari lifted the carton off the table and filled their glasses.

"So start spilling."

"The juice?"

"More details on your consummate dream date." Tracy jabbed her fork in the air. "Every single morsel of information you can think of."

Shari gave Tracy the highlights of the auction, the dance, the whole seduction process in general, her blue eyes growing nearly as starry as the aquamarine ones had been.

Tracy grinned like a smug little kitten as she doused her toast with syrup. "Wait until Magda hears how well her disguise worked—the walk, the talk, the makeup."

"Magda enjoys sleeping late on Sundays, but I'm sure she'll be around by the lunch hour with Broadway's other show folk."

"It's been so fun, the three of us plotting to make you the irresistible and mysterious siren. And then to see you return a rousing success…" She paused, her round face screwed up in thought. "I now know how a mad scientist feels when his killer tomato conquers a city."

Shari would rather Tracy made a comparison to a chic Manhattan image maker, but let it go in the spirit of the project. "Fine, Trace, wallow to your heart's content." Her slender brows arched a fraction. "After today, though, we'll be letting the whole thing go. I went into this charade knowing that I would be only borrowing Garrett to fulfill a forbidden fantasy and that's that. It's over."

"You sure have steely nerves."

"I'll put those to better use today handling Dylan. Wait until he finds out I lost the key to my apartment on a ring from the Beanery. A welcome invitation for even the most dim-witted burglar. And then there's all the money I spent on the auction. The bidding went wild, Trace. I blew thirty of my forty-grand inheritance from Aunt Lucille."

"That much!" Tracy gasped.

"I think Auntie would have approved of my purchase, but Dylan, of course, would flip his lid."

"Without a doubt. That money was earmarked for Beanery renovations. He fully expects you to pay some high-buck decorator with it. What on earth are you going to do?"

Shari shrank in the bulky confines of her borrowed robe, her voice a mere peep. "Hit the trade schools for some quick and easy do-it-yourself lessons, maybe?"

4

"SHE'S LATE! ON A SUNDAY no less!"

Dylan Johnson charged through the Beanery at the stroke of ten, unlocking the coffee shop's glass door on West Forty-fifth. "Not on a slow Monday, oh, no." He reached into the window display, flipped a switch to light up the green open sign, then turned to glare at Tracy.

Tracy laughed. "Cool down, Dylan. Shari came in the back door with me. She just needed to run upstairs to her apartment to change clothes."

Dylan's face darkened further. "Where was she last night, anyhow?"

Tracy smiled broadly, drawing on the material they'd prepared during their subway ride. "She had a date with some new guy."

"All night long? My innocent baby sister?" He paused as he let the unsavory implications sink in. "I'll break the jerk in two."

"The date ran a little late, is all," Tracy recited dutifully. "They were in Greenwich Village at some nightclub. Shari was about to call it a night when she realized she'd misplaced her keys. Since I live in the neighborhood, she came to get my spare. I convinced her to crash with me till morning." Tracy made a whisking motion with her hand, coming up for air. "Very simple, really."

Dylan, obsessively protective and practical, couldn't let it go so easily. "Why didn't she just come straight home and knock on my door? I live upstairs, too, right across the hall, with rings and rings of keys to every door in this building."

"She didn't want to disturb you."

"Since when?"

Tracy's full cheeks dimpled. The naive chump. Sure, Shari gave him fits sometimes just for sport, but her alter ego Flame would have given him cardiac arrest!

Dylan placed his hands at his waist, leaning into the service counter until he could breathe Tracy's air. "Are you laughing at me?"

"My lips aren't even moving."

"I mean inside, the way you girls tend to do when I spill something or forget an order."

"Hey, partner, the girl can't help it."

Dylan spun on his heel at the sound of Shari's voice. So wound up, he hadn't even heard her on the private staircase.

"Finally." Dylan advanced. "Be warned, Tracy told me everything about last night."

Shari highly doubted it. She smirked as Dylan assessed her for any open signs of damage, fairly confident that she'd completely transformed herself back into the mild-mannered, safe-looking sibling that pleased her brother so.

Behind her smirk, however, were new and unexpected traces of regret. Staring into the full-length mirror in the quiet of her own bedroom, Shari was hit hard by her familiar reflection. She'd thoroughly enjoyed being the irrepressible Flame and was clearly mourning her alter ego's demise.

Despite the lecture she'd given Tracy about the Cinderella trip being over, Shari held the hope that some of Flame's dazzle would translate back into her ordinary existence. But the mirror didn't lie. All traces of the wild, impetuous spirit were indeed snuffed out, from the pale hair rinsed of its metallic hue to the blue eyes no longer sparked by green contact lenses and the ivory complexion scrubbed free of stage makeup. Even the slender curves that had so nicely filled the red beaded dress were hidden beneath baggy Kelly-green T-shirt and jeans.

Your average plain Jane, stripped of her vampish energy.

Dylan's ideal image for her, she knew. Even so, her brother continued to fret over her safety and well-being. Ever since their folks had retired to Miami two years ago, Dylan had taken it upon himself to play her guardian tormentor full-time. So busy transforming the shop into a trendy singles hangout, Shari hadn't even considered misbehaving. Until last night. Last night made up for all the months of bickering and toiling.

"I thought we agreed, Shari, no Saturday-night dates for us."

"Dylan, you've got too many policies hammered into place. Mom and Dad ran this place for decades without policies."

He was taken aback by the complaint, which was not in keeping with her normally complacent nature. "The folks did fine, but we've taken this place way beyond their java-sandwich pit stop."

"But they worked hard, too, and somehow made time to go to the movies once in a while."

"But traffic is way up on the weekends because of our Club Wed dating service. You know single professionals don't have long enough lunch hours during the work-week to play the game properly. It takes time to study the postings on the bulletin board, collect mail from one's own posting."

Shari huffed in disgust. It was at times like this, when

Dylan was in full entrepreneurial gear, that she regretted her part in creating their busy matchmaking service.

Club Wed was an idea that sprouted a couple of years ago in a general conversation on how to renew the shop. The Beanery had been a neighborhood mainstay for ages, efficiently run by the Johnsons. It was with sadness, however, that Shari and Dylan watched profits and quality begin to slide with time. The number of original patrons had started to dwindle and more strangers jammed the place for take-out snacks, moving in and out so fast that it was impossible to put a name with a face.

Their parents' retirement to Florida seemed the ideal occasion to breathe new life into the shop. Shari and Dylan took over the reins with open minds and gusto, resuscitating the menu with trendy coffees, low-fat sandwiches and more packaged snacks.

This first phase proved a success, drawing in crowds of young professionals and artists looking for healthy fare. Encouraged, they set higher goals, plotting a full renovation of the shop's interior and some kind of a social icebreaker that would keep the new wave of yuppies eating their improved menu on-site, where they could mingle and ask for seconds.

They'd mulled over schemes ranging from eat-with-a-stranger to name-that-stranger. Nothing seemed to click. Then Shari decided a customer survey might better open their eyes to patrons' needs. The information collected proved invaluable. Seemed most of their patrons were single and yearned to find a mate. So the brother-sister duo settled upon a romantic theme and Club Wed was born.

"Shari, that glare is going to freeze on your face," Dylan threatened, bringing her out of her funk.

"Does it matter what I look like when I have no personal life of my own?"

Dylan was taken aback by her words. His sister rarely complained about the hours dedicated to the shop. "What's your hurry, Shari? You're only twenty-five."

"Almost twenty-six. Anyway, you'll be using that tone when I'm *ninety*-five, I bet."

"Now, that's silly," he muttered.

Shari poked her brother's thick biceps. "Just because you have no interest in romance doesn't mean I—"

Dylan looked frantically at the entrance. "Hush up. What will customers think if they catch the operators of Club Wed arguing about romance?"

"Someone with a B.A. in literature from Columbia should be more sensitive about these things," Shari argued.

"I'm sensitive," he snapped in contradiction, drawing laughter from Tracy. "You know I got that particular degree especially so I'd have something to think about while running this shop, something to talk about with the customers. If we hope to make it big, every move we make should revolve around this business venture."

Shari had never wholeheartedly agreed with that theory. In fact, she'd gotten a degree in business administration so she could someday explore a world beyond the coffee shop. It was a difference between the siblings that called for tolerance. But Shari wasn't feeling especially patient since letting go with Garrett. A taste of fulfillment, a real glimpse of the world beyond this place left her more hungry and ambitious than she'd been before.

"Try to understand my point here," she pleaded. "If we continue to bury ourselves strictly in our work, we'll never find personal happiness."

"I have noticed you've seemed restless the past few weeks, but I thought maybe it was the spring weather."

"Oh, Dylan, despite your education, you have no interest in expanding your horizons. Just because Allison

Walker didn't pledge her heart and soul to you after high school graduation—"

"Knock it off about Allison. You know better."

"But that's what is really stopping you from giving your heart again. You've never truly cared about another girl since. Say," she said with inspiration, "why don't you go ahead and try our dating service once, Dylan. Think of it as a publicity stunt." Shari turned to Tracy. "We'll all try it. Give the customers a show."

Dylan's normally ruddy complexion went white as he struggled for an excuse. "Aw, no. If we start dabbling in Club Wed ourselves, we'll get distracted, and tie up customers who could be discovering true love elsewhere."

Shari raised her chin defiantly. "Everyone deserves a shot at true love. Even me."

"You will have it," Dylan assured her. "Someday. But in the meantime, don't harass the customers by trying to date them."

Her eyes narrowed. "I can if I want to."

Dylan eyed her suspiciously. "Hey, is the guy you were with last night from the Club Wed system? Did you dip into the well already?"

"No, of course not."

Dylan remained concerned. "Is he the kind of guy you could get serious about?"

Memories of Garrett, the hopelessness of their future together took some of the starch out of her. "No, he's definitely not husband material."

Dylan couldn't disguise his relief. "Gee. Better luck next time."

"Yeah, sure."

He tapped her nose. "Take my advice and keep the old sniffer to the grindstone for now. What with the forty grand apiece we inherited from Aunt Lucille, we finally have the chance to spruce this place up properly. We have to focus to do it right."

Nervous about where this even more volatile subject might lead, Shari moved away to fluff some pillows on the worn velvet sofa in the far corner of the shop.

Business was brisk for the next hour, keeping the staff on their toes. Shari and one of their college-age servers waited tables while Dylan and Tracy worked the counter.

Shari was delighted to spot her fairy godmother of the night, Magda DuCharme, floating in about noon, dressed in flowing Gypsyish pants and blouse of violet and lavender and laden with gold jewelry, most of which was bought on the street.

Magda was an enigma to all who knew her, regal yet unconventional, aged yet timeless. A Broadway actress versus starlet in her prime, she was practical about the craft of acting, the modest salaries and billing she'd received over the course of her career. She was quite practical about everything, with the exception of romance. Shari dreamed up the concept for her fantasy night, but it was Magda who insisted she follow through, using all her skills in makeup and method acting to prep Shari for the role of Flame.

Magda greeted many patrons, as was her way, but her pointed look landed squarely on Shari. She wanted the facts on Flame's derring-do.

Shari directed Magda to one of the few available tables, located in the back, its view obstructed by the display case. It was frequently empty because eager singles couldn't clearly see the door from it. Despite Dylan's objections to her sudden lunch break, Shari prepared a tray for two, consisting of cappuccinos and thick turkey sandwiches. Tracy took over her share of the waitressing duties, lingering at the table to gauge Magda's reaction to Shari's good review.

One look at Shari's radiant face across the table and the thin, expressive woman cried out joyfully, leaning over the table to clasp her protégée's cheeks. "I am so proud. Not everyone could pull off such a demanding role. But you, Shari, with your quick wit and lusty appetites—"

"Mags!" Shari slanted a worried look to the counter, where Dylan was busily mixing together cherry Italian sodas.

Magda gave her cheek one last pat, then settled back. "Oh, never mind about your brother. All he can hear is the jingle of coin around here. Weeks of preparation for last night's auction and he noticed nothing."

"That's true," Shari agreed, sipping coffee from her oversize cup.

Magda attacked her sandwich hungrily, speaking between bites. "So tell me everything, from start to finish."

Shari spoke in a conspiratorial whisper, going on in length about the yacht, the clothes, things that she knew the actress would appreciate most.

Magda had closed her plum-shadowed eyes, visualizing each nuance. She opened them now, though, to meet Shari's gaze squarely. "It sounds truly blissful. As long as he was a most satisfying lover."

Shari blushed, tucking strands of pale hair behind her ears. "Most definitely."

"Then it was well worth all the effort," Magda crowed. "Good sex is hard to come by."

Tracy was still standing by, clutching her order pad to her chest with a wistful look. "Isn't that the truth?"

Dylan hit the bell on the order counter with a rapid ping-ping motion. "Food's up, Tracy! What are you waiting for, girl?"

"Good sex would be nice for starters," she grumbled to the pair before flouncing off.

Magda beamed proudly. "Your best friend, she is jealous. The ultimate compliment to a fine performance."

Shari considered her tryst with Garrett something far more meaningful than a performance, but didn't object. She was well accustomed to the way Magda viewed the whole world as a stage and the general population the thespian's fodder.

Besides, no one on earth could truly understand how desperately in love Shari had been with Garrett during her formative years, how tough it had been to stand before him day after day in this very shop, all but invisible as he flirted with girls his own age. How she'd dreamed of someday, some way, getting a taste of that smooth McNamara action.

Magda went on airily. "Reminds me of my early days in repertoire. Knowing your company on some levels, but unsure what they'd pull out of a hat during a live performance. Anything could and did happen." She feigned disgust. "Improvisational cads."

"Now, Mags," Shari teased, "you talking on- or off-stage?"

Magda boomed with husky laughter. "Both!"

Feeling a fresh rush of gratitude, Shari impulsively reached over and gave the woman's bejeweled hands a quick squeeze. "One last time, I want to thank you for stepping in as my producer."

"Haven't had so much fun in years," Magda assured her. "Why, in no time, I could be coaxed into orchestrating a sequel."

"Oh, no," Shari cautioned. "The curtain is down for good on this one."

Magda shook her head with a click of her tongue. "Mags can see right through your protests. There remains a hunger in your face, on that high dizzy level just above the fine chocolate craving."

Shari did indeed find herself with a lingering feeling in a very intimate place. If possible, sex with her childhood crush had been too powerful, too fulfilling. For those long, heated hours aboard the suitably named *Temptation*, she'd actually come to own him body and soul.

Certainly a headier passion than she had dared anticipate even in her wildest imaginings.

Or dared forget, it seemed.

Sitting here calmly with a decent meal, Shari was just coming to measure the extent of her yearnings. What a cruel trick of nature that she'd awakened in his bed faced with an incredible yen for an erotic encore. But through her fevered haze she'd realized that the risk of discovery would be much higher in the harsh light of day. All that stood between the tousled and smudged Flame and little Shari Johnson was a good scrub with soap and water.

It would have all been disastrous had he come to realize exactly who and what she was. It was smarter to cut the cord cleanly and catch a ride with the catering crew, who were too tired and disinterested to care that she was already a shadow of her former self, a recycled Cinderella best suited to a pumpkin ride home.

Magda carefully watched the pensive Shari, growing smugger by the second. "You see, in matters of amour, I know you better than you know yourself."

"No way," Shari said flatly. "I have nothing left to bankroll another project. Between the thirty-grand bid and the two-grand dress, I'm left with under ten grand in my account. It will have to be stretched to impossible lengths once the renovation gears up."

Magda was an artist in the purest form, with limited understanding of the practical. "Perhaps you could replenish the account," she gushed naively. "Get into some crap game, perhaps."

Shari realized the idea was straight out of *Guys and Dolls*. "I'm no Sky Masterson, so forget it."

She clutched her bosom with a wounded gesture. "As you wish."

"Oh, I don't know what I wish anymore," Shari grumbled, rubbing the tender skin beneath her wire-rim glasses.

"Eat your sandwich." Magda gestured to her plate. "I always look like a glutton when you pick-pick that way."

WALKING INTO THE BEANERY that afternoon had a more profound effect on Garrett than he would have dreamed possible. It was like entering another dimension, rediscovering a life lost, slipping back into a very comfortable zone.

So much remained the same. The U-shaped central workstation was head-on, with its boxy display case, counter and cash register. Tables and shelves behind the case boasted a variety of small appliances, mostly coffeemakers, old and new.

Off to the left stood the familiar stainless steel tables and booths with pumpkin-colored Formica tops and cushioned seats upholstered in black vinyl.

On the right side of the shop a hodgepodge of odd furniture, overstuffed chairs and wooden straightbacks, made up a new and inviting adult-friendly area. During his senior-high days, this space was geared toward the younger customer, with pinball machines and candy dispensers. He fondly pictured the teenage version of himself standing at his favorite baseball machine with a can of soda and a roast beef on rye in hand, harassing his fellow basketball players, teasing Dylan's kid sister.

Something behind the furniture caught Garrett's eye next: a giant oak-framed bulletin board full of pastel index cards hanging on the wall above a substantial ledge in matching oak. On the ledge sat a stack of envelopes and notepaper, as well as a hinged wooden box with a slit in its cover. A banner of calligraphy hung overhead, pronouncing this Club Wed territory.

It reminded Garrett of a Valentine's Day display out of school. This was far more sophisticated, though, judging by the quality of the banner and the well-turned-out patrons gathered round. Probably was some kind of lavish gimmick, if he knew his old pal Dylan.

The biggest surprise of all was the look of those patrons. Thirteen years ago, this place was a modest family coffee shop, a hangout for teenagers and stop-off for parents in need of a quick take-out meal of sandwiches. Today it swelled with affluent yuppies and chic artist types.

He turned back to the counter, catching a pretty woman several years his junior sizing him up with interest. She was cute in a clean, refreshing way, with long, straight black hair and a round, dimpled face, dressed in soft jeans and a tight Kelly-green T-shirt. But she was no Flame, and that's all he could think of today. Memories of their night together were branded into his mind. Her whole scheme had been such a kick, her lovemaking an exhilarating joyride.

He would tear Manhattan down brick by brick to find her. Plain and simple.

"I'm Tracy," the pretty young thing said. "Can I help you?"

Garrett sauntered over, shoving his hands in the pockets of his cashmere slacks. "Nice to meet you, Tracy. I'm looking for Dylan. He still loaf around this place?"

Dylan heard the exchange as he was emerging from

the back room with a rack of cups fresh out of the dish-washer. "Hey, man! Who let a renegade like you in here!" Quickly setting down the rack on a work counter, he dashed around the display case.

"Bet that's the fastest you've moved since the basket-ball tourney against Washington High."

The men hesitated between a handshake and a hug, causing Tracy to intervene dryly. "Bet you boys were all over each other after a winning game. Go ahead."

The pair embraced with hearty chuckles. As they broke apart, Dylan gave Garrett a punch in the biceps, the way he used to do to check his muscle mass. His arm was still as solid as his own.

"Believe it or not, buddy, I'm running this place now."

Garrett looked visibly impressed. "Really? So the folks did go ahead and retire?"

"Yeah, Mom and Pop were off for sunny pastures two years ago." Dylan turned back to the counter to snap an order at Tracy. "Hey, hand over a couple of Mountain Dews."

"Yes, mein leader." With a click of her heels Tracy reached into the display case and set two cans of soda on top.

"This guy was a best friend back in school," Dylan told her proudly.

"I figured that out," Tracy drawled with little interest.

"The backbone of our B-ball team. The forward we could count on to make the most points."

Garrett flushed with pleasure. "Couldn't have made all those shots without guards like you."

Tracy laughed as she addressed their visitor. "We go through this spiel with every old buddy who pops in here. Dylan's baiting you for compliments."

"I do that sometimes," Dylan admitted. "But this guy

is really special, Tracy. One of the bigger success stories in my old crowd."

"You don't say." Tracy tossed her thick black mane over her shoulders, sizing up their visitor more boldly.

"We've both done all right." Garrett would have preferred coffee to the sweet citrus drink but cracked open the can, anyway, just for old times' sake. "And I think we settled that a few years back at our ten-year class reunion."

"So we did. Since then I've made some of the changes I told you about. Got rid of the kid stuff. Seemed best as kids stopped coming in. And there's more improvements in the works. Remember my old aunt Lucille who made those giant cookies for the shop? She died a few months back and left Shari and me some money. We've been using it to buy the best of everything. Started off with state-of-the art coffee machines, a bigger refrigerator and cupboard space in back."

"So you know Shari, too?" Tracy interrupted in surprise.

"Why, yes," Garrett replied fondly. "She was always scampering around underfoot."

"Still is underfoot," Dylan mumbled dismissively. "As I was saying, the real work is planned for this summer. We're having the plumbing and electrical updated, the tables and other furniture replaced." His voice dropped a notch, full of reverence. "Our customers are so upscale these days. We want to bring the place up to spec in keeping with the times, their expectations. Make a bundle of cash! Nothing in your league, of course."

"It's a fine plan." Garrett's gaze wandered again with a fixed smile as he imagined a social barrier climbing from the old tiled flooring. Damn, he didn't want to be set apart from Dylan now any more than he wanted it way back when. His late father, Brent, had been behind

Garrett attending the modest high school because of their superb mathematics and sports programs. How Brent had loved basketball! And Garrett had for the most part enjoyed those years. But he'd thought there'd always been an undercurrent among the few kids who resented his wealth. It still hurt him to this day.

There was no denying, of course, that he fit the upscale profile that still awed his pal, despite his deliberate attempt to tone down in gray slacks and pale blue polo shirt. Clearly, sparing the tie hadn't been near enough to bring him into his fair-haired friend's middle-class circle. There were all the little details that were so much a part of Garrett: jet hair styled in a sleek executive trim, hand-sewn loafers, jeweled watch. Dylan was still easygoing shaggy from his fair hair to his worn hip-hugging jeans and Kelly-green Beanery T-shirt.

Garrett knew better than to try to convince Dylan that he'd always envied him to some degree for his simple approach to people, his automatic trust in them. From the start, Dylan figured Garrett had it made in life with all the perks of an affluent family. What Dylan didn't take into account was that he was doing his longing from the safety of his warm and loving family. Garrett had paid an emotional price for his family's wealth and lofty social position with a cool and controlling mother who judged people by narrow and rigid standards; who had, quite justly, cautioned Garrett to keep distance from people until he was sure they weren't out to use him somehow.

At least Garrett didn't have to worry about a Johnson using him. He and Dylan had always been good friends. Why, the whole family had treated him well.

Not wanting the silence between them to grow awkward, Garrett spoke up. "Probably should've dropped in right after the reunion, like you told me to."

Dylan slapped him on the back. "It's time wasted, pure and simple."

Garrett almost said that Dylan could have called him, too, but the old crowd never did, figuring Garrett was too out of reach. "Well, life's been hectic," he claimed casually.

"Aw, never mind. Anytime's good to catch up on old times."

"Or enjoy new times. Dyl, I've come because I have a puzzle that needs solving." Garrett removed a hand from his pocket. In his palm he held the scuffed shop key ring holding a single key. "I'm trying to find the owner of this. Think you can help me?"

Dylan snorted in good humor. "We only hand them out like candy." He made a move to handle it, but Garrett closed his palm in a covetous way.

Tracy made a squeaky sound behind the counter, her expression shifting to panic. "Gee, you find that on the street or something?"

"Not exactly..."

Tracy couldn't help adding up the small hints that this might be a very significant visitor indeed. She extended her hand over a stack of napkins. "I'm Tracy."

"So you told me," Garrett said politely.

"And you are?" she pressed shamelessly.

Dylan huffed in exasperation. "Down, girl."

"The name is Garrett McNamara." He shook her hand, finding it strangely limp. "You all right?"

Tracy nodded, dazed. "Fine."

Dylan stood by, hands on the waistband of his jeans. "So, Garrett, what's the deal with this key ring?"

"I spent the night with the most enchanting goddess imaginable," he confided. "This is the only clue she left behind to her identity."

Tracy stole a look back to the rear of the shop where

Shari and Magda were blissfully finishing off their sand-wiches, then whirled back breathlessly. "And what would you want her for, Garrett? If you don't mind my asking."

"He would mind, nosy," Dylan said dismissively. "So fill me in properly here, buddy. How could you spend the night with a goddess, unsure of who she is?"

Garrett reddened, avoiding Tracy's watchful eye. "It was sort of an adult game, guess you could say. I was auctioned off at the Waldorf last night—"

"Oh, that's right! I did see you in the Bachelor Auction brochure," Dylan confirmed. "We encouraged partici-pation by our customers. The high rollers, anyway."

"Yes, well, this goddess was my highest bidder." Gar-rett's eyes twinkled. "Insisted upon keeping her identity a secret through the entire night, no matter how I coaxed."

Dylan wiggled his golden brows. "That does sound like a real turn-on."

"It was. For the night. But now that the date is offi-cially over, I want to get to know her better."

"Funny, an operator like you letting her slip through your fingers."

"Well," Garrett grumbled, "I was asleep aboard the *Temptation* at the time."

Dylan guffawed loudly. "You oaf."

"Shut up," Garrett hissed, glancing around the shop at several curious patrons balancing coffee cups. "The whole world will know in a minute."

"Okay, sorry." Dylan gulped for air. "But I can't help but be amazed by the whole thing."

"Because you have no love life of your own, maybe?" Tracy sniped.

"No, because it isn't at all like Garrett here. He's al-ways been pretty reserved, private. Nothing made him angrier than his mother trying to screen the cheerleaders he dated." Dylan gave his friend a measured look. "Hey, this kind of extravaganza smacks of her kind of interference."

Garrett felt a tightening in his chest. He should have known that Dylan would put him on the rack for every detail. "Yes, Gwen roped me in. But I didn't figure that out until later, and by then I was enjoying myself. Besides, it was all for a good cause."

"Sure, man, sure. So how did it feel? I mean, being bought that way."

"Liked it more than I expected to," Garrett happily admitted.

Never truly smitten by anything but a picture of Ben Franklin on a bill, Dylan asked his most nagging question. "How much, man? How much did you cost?"

Garrett rubbed his neck and shifted position. "Does that matter?"

"C'mon, tell me."

"Thirty thousand."

"What!" Dylan snagged his arm, brimming with excitement. "This is too incredible not to share."

"With who?"

"Only my baby sister. She's right back here at a table goofing off. Go get her, Tracy."

Tracy's mouth opened. "But—but—but—"

Dylan pushed her chin up to close her mouth. "Just go. Tell her I have a big surprise."

5

"TRACY, I DON'T CARE if Dylan wants me." Shari huffed in exasperation, staring up at her friend. "My lunch hour runs another seven minutes."

Tracy made a high funny sound as she hovered over the table. "The plan, the performance. Busted. Kaput."

Magda drained her coffee. "I think you should sit down before you go into orbit."

"I can't, Mags. But Shari should—"

"Hey, Shari!" Dylan called, drowning out Tracy's protests.

Tracy danced on tiptoe. "Don't say I didn't warn you." With that she turned and left.

Garrett shifted uncomfortably from one loafer to another as Dylan called to his sister a second time. He hoped to elicit help without giving out his story to the general public. But Shari wasn't the public, was she? Garrett remembered her as a skinny little pest always underfoot, the team mascot, everyone's surrogate baby sister. And who knew, maybe she knew Flame.

Within moments he spotted Shari wending through tables between Tracy and an older woman. A grown-up version of a pert little blonde he remembered quite vividly. The braids were gone, but she still had the same kid-sister quality about her: clear complexion with only a trace of lipstick, a thin body draped with loose jeans, Kelly T-shirt and baggy work shirt. Exactly what he'd expect of Shari.

"Huh?" Shari froze in her tracks, her china-blue eyes widening behind her lenses like a disbelieving child. "You, Garrett? You're the surprise?"

"Isn't this too much, sis?" Dylan raved. "I bet never in your wildest dreams did you expect to see successful financier Garrett McNamara standing here—in our humble place."

Shari froze in time and space. *Wild* was the word for her dreams, all right, the wildest imaginable. Far more than Dylan realized. She'd dared to do what millions of other women would never attempt: she'd put those dreams in motion. How shortsighted of her to think there'd be no consequences, that she'd never have to face him again.

Boldly returning his stare, Shari found herself lost in the depths of his gray eyes all over again. Images of last night flashed to vivid life, his lips on her skin, his flesh deep inside her. She quivered under her baggy clothes, wondering if he could feel the energy humming between them.

Garrett felt a twinge deep in his subconscious as they locked eyes. There was something rather magical in her expression. He couldn't quite pinpoint it, for it belied her meek appearance. But she'd always been the playful kind, reassuringly harmless, as dependable as a puppy. He was just drawn to her innate warmth, that was all.

"You'll never guess why Garrett's here," Tracy said, nudging her.

"You see, sis," Dylan interjected, "Garrett was involved in that bachelor auction last night."

Shari averted her gaze from Garrett's then, digging a tennis shoe into the floor.

"He was sold off for thirty grand! Can you imagine."

"Wow."

"Yeah, the rich really know how to live in this city."

Dylan paused to marvel over such foibles. "Anyway, his date was playing the mystery woman with him, but he managed to trace her here, to us."

Shari's heart flipped. "How?"

"With a Beanery key ring. His date left it behind."

"Imagine that." So that's what happened to her apartment key!

Magda closed in with a flourish of violet chiffon, her aged face alive with curiosity. She surveyed their visitor with her standard footlight squint. "You are *the* Garrett McNamara?"

"I'm the only one I know of," he replied.

"Do you like sequels, Mr. McNamara?"

Garrett's brows crunched in perplexity. "I don't understand."

Shari slanted Magda a warning frown. "You'll have to excuse Mags, Garrett. She's theater down to the toenails and likes to ask irrelevant questions just to look stylishly eccentric."

Magda cackled. "Irrelevance is all in the eye of the beholder."

"I was just about to explain," Dylan said, "that Garrett's date is probably a member of Club Wed."

"How do you make that leap in judgment?" Tracy demanded.

"Because all the singles enrolled in the dating service seem to be using our key rings for their apartment keys. This mysterious ring has a single key that looks very much like the kind used in this very building in fact—in buildings for miles around." Dylan suddenly realized that Garrett and Shari were still joined in a trance for two. "Is something the matter, Garrett? Shari got some leaf lettuce caught between her teeth or something?"

Shari gasped in horror. "Dylan Johnson!"

"I was just thinking, Shari…" Garrett mused, tapping

his lips with a finger. "There's something significant about you teasing the back of my mind."

"Ohmigod," Tracy squealed.

Shari pinkened, disturbed in a tantalizing way. She hadn't counted on Garrett finding her out. Ever. Their lives were hopelessly divided by about a hundred million dollars and several tiers of society. But now, mere hours later, a simple mislaid key had landed him here full of questions.

"It's been teasing at me," he said with a slow, deliberate nod.

"What?"

"A particular nickname, I think."

Shari recognized that look, inquisitive and sexy, giving his lean, angled features a playfulness. He'd looked exactly the same way before he'd entered her for the first time last night. Quaking under her baggy clothes, Shari raised her slender hands in protest. "Now, Garrett, it might not be such a good thing to just blurt something out."

"You are going to own up, aren't you?"

"I'd rather not."

He snapped his fingers triumphantly. "Oh, I've got it now!"

Shari cringed, leaning against the side of the glass case holding pastries. "I wish you wouldn't *say* anything."

He leaned close, his gray eyes merry. "But the String Bean is such a cute name."

"The String Bean!" Her shriek caused Garrett to jump.

"Yeah, it was sitting there on the tip of my tongue all the time."

Huh. She hadn't noticed it on his tongue last night.

He beamed at her, as if to coax back her smile. "Surely there must be a few diehards who still call you that."

"Not a one." She stood erectly, her dignity giving her

more height than her five-foot-three frame generally allowed.

"Sorry, I'd never purposely give you heat."

Therein lay the problem, Shari fumed, feeling more letdown than she should. Garrett wouldn't even consider heating up for Shari Johnson, while he'd delight in building a forest fire with Flame.

Still, there was a simmer in Garrett's gaze. Something on some level clicked, as though Garrett spotted a flicker of intrigue in her and was trying to sort it out. But he wasn't even close to understanding it and she should be relieved.

This sudden twist of fate was so unfair. She'd gone into the night knowing it was one temporary encounter, meant to be filed away in her memory, dusted off on occasion for her own private pleasure. How was she expected to move on with the object of her most wanton desires hanging around her place of business, a candid reminder that she didn't hold a candle to Flame in real life?

As he stood smack-dab in the middle of her space, Shari felt a quiver of spunk, the urge to reveal herself, forcing him to deal with it. But that rush of power would last mere seconds, and a plausible explanation would then be in order. In the fallout, she'd be left with the burden of proving herself that captivating creature and would undoubtedly have to jump through some embarrassing hoops, only to ultimately deal with his disappointment.

It would do to keep in mind that he was bound to be let down by such a mundane answer to his mystery. Flame was a fantasy come to life, who put games of seduction at the top of her list, who spent money on men like so much water. Save for this one splurge, Shari spent her money on life's necessities, spent her time tending this shop. Not the image to capture a millionaire jet-setter like Garrett McNamara.

It would also do well to anticipate her brother's foul reaction to her wild spending spree, to the hole it left in their renovation budget.

"The String Bean," Dylan repeated fiendishly. "There's a tag worth resurrecting."

"Don't you dare," Shari threatened.

Garrett smiled unsteadily at Shari, not sure exactly what had snapped the line of electricity running between them. But he felt a surprising sense of loss. "I'm looking for a little help," he ventured awkwardly.

"Yes, yes," Dylan agreed. "I think we can hook you up with Flame. May take a little time, but the Club Wed system is bound to be the answer."

"Exactly what is Club Wed?" Garrett asked. "I noticed the setup over there."

"Remember that scam we ran back in school, setting up dates for school functions?"

"Sure, the cash got you to basketball camp a couple of summers."

"It's the grown-up version, guess you could say." Dylan paused as he noticed a bakery truck rolling up outside. "I've told that guy a hundred times to go around back," he complained, heading for the front door. "Shari will show you the ropes, Garrett. Be right back."

Garrett hesitated. "Do you mind, Shari?"

"I suppose not." With a tight smile she eased by him and moved through the main area of the shop to the matchmaking station.

They stood together at the bulletin board among several other patrons. Garrett was a bit anxious, and not just about his search. Shari had always meant a lot to him and he didn't want to upset her in any way. "Hey, I'm sorry about the name...."

"It's fine. Really."

"It just leapt to mind."

Shari couldn't contain her exasperation. "If memory serves me right, Garrett, you were one of the precious few who didn't taunt me about that name."

He had the grace to look sheepish. "Guess that's true, isn't it?"

"Yes."

"It won't happen again."

"Good. Now, about Club Wed..." Thoughtful, Shari gathered up her thick hair in her fingers, revealing a glimpse of shapely neck before sending the buttery mane rippling between her shoulder blades.

The movement rippled Garrett's subconscious. Flame had done the same thing a couple of times as she moved through the cabin gloriously naked. Apparently hair rippling must be a habit shared by much of the female population. With a slight frown he concentrated on Shari's pitch, which was suddenly more formal.

"Guess the club is best described as a dating service for lonely Manhattan singles serious about finding a marriage partner. It caters mainly to busy professionals who have limited time to hunt."

"The clientele sure has changed around here."

She brightened with pride. "Yes, we noticed a gradual upscale transition even before the folks turned over the reins. That was when Dylan and I got to thinking that we could capitalize on it if we were smart. The idea was to bring patrons together in a cozy environment in contrast to the impersonal city streets. We removed the pinball machines, added the furniture and set about formulating a getting-acquainted gimmick. Club Wed was the result. It's been a big hit since the beginning."

He scanned the board crowded with three-by-five-inch pastel index cards. "Pink cards for the ladies, blue ones for the guys?"

"Right. We've found the visual distinction makes perusal much easier." She tapped a pink card with her index finger, noting a trace of glue from last night's false fingernails on her cuticle. It gave her pause, but only for half a beat. Garrett wouldn't know what it was. "As you can see, we've had them custom-printed with headings so our members can fill them in and read about others with the same ease."

Garrett was impressed with the setup. Under the Name heading, each card listed a first name and a four-digit code. Joan 0097, Amanda 1035. Other headings included Age, Interests, Profession. The bottom was reserved for the heading, Requirements Sought In Mate.

His thoughts turned exclusively to Flame. For all he knew, she could very well be represented on this board, hidden behind her true name. Was she a Joan or an Emily or a Kelsey? And how did she envision her perfect man?

Shari watched him inspect the cards with a disgustingly hungry expression. She struggled for professional distance.

"So how do I go about communicating with the ladies on the board?"

Her heart squeezed painfully at the very idea. Still, she launched into the procedure as she had dozens of times to newcomers, running a hand over the inexpensive buff stationery on the shelf. "If one club member wishes to communicate with another on the board, he composes a message on one of these note cards, slips it in one of these envelopes with the addressee's first name and code number in the center, his in the top left corner." She gave the wooden box a pat. "Then it's deposited in here. We empty the box twice a day—once at noon, once at closing. Finally the envelopes are sorted and held for pickup. Members can check with any employee to see if they have mail."

Garrett was disgustingly excited. "So how do I join up?"

"Come over to the register and I'll get you a blue index card to fill out."

Shari led the way back to the store's central hub, where Tracy was manning the register and borderline-diabetic Magda was supposedly selecting some giant bakery cookies. Obviously they'd anticipated Garrett's registration and were stationed to witness the event, Shari realized. The insatiable eavesdroppers.

Tracy pushed a pen and blue index card over the glass with a teasing wink. "Is this the right order, mister?"

Garrett accepted them with a chuckle. "So how much is Dylan soaking his members for? Do they pay by the message or what? Knowing my buddy the way I do, he has to be coming out of this pretty sweet."

Shari had rounded the case to stand beside Tracy. The barrier of glass and steel between her and this infuriating man gave her the nerve to get sassy. "We charge thirty grand to our best customers."

He laughed harder, reaching out to tap her nose with the pen. "C'mon now, seriously."

Shocked by Shari's taunt, Tracy jumped in to referee. "There's a one time registration fee of thirty dollars. After that, there's a twenty-dollar-a-month service fee."

"Sounds like a bargain." He filled in the card, which Shari took charge of.

"I'll post this right away," she promised, resisting the urge to crumple it in her hand, "and give you a smaller membership identification card. Whenever you want your mail, you hand any clerk here your ID."

"Great. Perfect." Garrett opened his wallet and paid Tracy.

Shari reached into a plastic box beside the register for a white ID card about the size of a driver's license and filled in Garrett's name and number. Unable to actually bring herself to give him his official entrée to the club, she handed it to Tracy, who passed it along with his change.

"I do feel it only fair to warn you, Garrett," Shari said with some satisfaction, "that Flame might not even be a member of the club."

Garrett leaned closer, inviting their confidence. "In or out of the club, I'm betting at least one of you three already knows Flame."

Shari glanced at Tracy and Magda with a gasp. "Maybe, but if she was in disguise—"

Garrett's brows rose a fraction. "Ah, but I did pick up some hints to her true identity."

Tracy feigned amazement. "Do tell."

"For starters, she's well versed in the arts and an excellent dancer."

Magda pretended to scour her memory. "That covers so many patrons."

"Then there's the deft way she handled my very difficult mother. I'd say she qualifies as the ultimate diplomat."

"Diplomats don't come in here much," Shari scoffed.

He smiled wryly. "I was only speaking metaphorically, of course. Her true profession is in the import-export business. That useful nugget slipped out in general conversation. I doubt she even realized it."

Magda's plum lips curved. "The import-export business you say. How exciting. Doesn't that sound exciting, Tracy?"

"Very."

Shari found the playful conversation remarkably agitating. She gratefully noted two customers scanning for a table. "I must get back to work. Nice seeing you, Garrett."

"THE IMPORT-EXPORT BUSINESS?" Tracy's voice was a rude hoot as she and Shari strolled through Central Park later that sunny afternoon. "That's a funny lie to tell."

"It wasn't a lie!" Shari protested impishly. "Our coffee at the shop is from South America, that's an import."

"And exports?"

"Well…" Shari bit her lip. "I take out the trash all the time. That counts as an export."

"Wow, I never knew you were such a sneak."

"I felt trapped," Shari admitted flatly. "Crowded into that fancy limo with those solid gold socialites. I had to say something impressive."

"I suppose so." Tracy paused to admire a couple of male joggers passing by. To her chagrin, Shari didn't join in. "What's with you, anyway? Those guys were smiling back at me. They might have stopped if you'd given them some encouragement."

"My heart isn't in it today."

"Oh, don't tell me I've got a lovesick fool on my hands now."

"I'm not a fool."

"C'mon, we need to talk this over." Tracy hauled her over to an empty park bench for a sit-down cross-examination.

Shari shifted on the bench, averting her gaze. "I need some time to forget Garrett, that's all."

"Hon, Garrett was just for the night. You knew that going in. You planned it that way."

Shari sniffed. "Sure, but I didn't think he'd show up at the shop within hours. Wanting me—"

"Wanting Flame, you mean, the exotic, carefree siren of Manhattan. A woman of his class who can dazzle his family and friends, produce babies with rich blue blood pouring through their veins."

"But I'm a reasonable facsimile, the working-girl's version."

"He's so hot on her, though, he couldn't see anything or anyone else."

Shari twisted her hands in her lap. "Okay, so one look at me didn't make his heart skip."

"C'mon, he looks at you and thinks of skipping rope."

"You are so cruel—but so right," she quickly conceded, hanging her head mournfully. "If only he hadn't tracked me down."

Tracy's dimples deepened. "You had to figure he might try and find Flame for a bit more hanky-panky. I mean, you pulled out all the stops to be irresistible."

"It occurred to me that he might make some surface inquiries, perhaps go to the auction organizers to trace me through my check—which is why I opened the Flame Unlimited account. But I didn't expect him to make a beeline to the shop, close in like a lusty Sherlock Holmes. Was it ever hard to take, watching my sweet prince of a lover staring right through me in his dream search."

"Guess if there was any lesson in the perils of a no-strings fling, this is it."

"No kidding," Shari grumbled. "What torture it will be if he starts to hang out at the Beanery again like in the old days, chumming up to Dylan, treating me like a gangly kid. I'll be a prisoner in my own place. Trapped by my duties, forced to watch him scour the city through my dating service."

"He'll eventually come to realize that Flame isn't a customer."

"Sure, and in the meantime he'll tap into every remote possibility, most likely find another suitable partner in the process."

Tracy gave her raven head a shake. "You've got to get a grip on yourself."

"How can I possibly survive falling from a glorious Venus status in his eyes to that of an innocuous Cupid?"

"That fall does seem cruel punishment for a little play-acting."

"Then there's the other punishment in store for me," Shari lamented. "When Dylan discovers that most of my share of Aunt Lucille's inheritance is gone, he'll explode."

"He'll probably come to realize that garnisheeing your wages for a year will cover it."

"What!" The very idea hadn't occurred to Shari and with any luck wouldn't occur to her brother, either. "Don't you dare say that again out loud. Don't even think it!"

Tracy shrugged. "All right, all right. Maybe with a little ingenuity you can somehow keep your dwindling funds a secret, too."

Shari balled her fists. "This is more pressure than I'm up for."

"Maybe Garrett will simmer down after a decent night's sleep and decide that finding Flame shouldn't be such a priority."

"I highly doubt it. Not when he's bothered to join Club Wed."

Tracy laughed indulgently. "Do you realize what you've done? You've made a millionaire hunk your love slave!"

Shari didn't even crack a smile. If only there was a future in it for them as a couple. But even in the best of circumstances, Garrett could never accept that she, the

String Bean, had rocked his world so completely. So now they were both sentenced to a form of lonely limbo, wanting their perfectly matched lover, dreaming an impossible dream. She covered her face with her hands. "I wish I could vanish for a few months, until he tires of the hunt."

Tracy scoffed at the idea. "It isn't like you to wimp out."

She dropped her hands to her knees. "What can I do to stop this?"

"You might consider contacting him through the club as Flame."

"And say what?"

"Get lost," Tracy suggested.

"But then he'd realize she frequents the shop and know for sure she's a member of the club. He could be all the more encouraged."

"So be firm in your rejection."

"But he's always liked a challenge. He might think it's another of Flame's ploys to keep him on the string."

Tracy sighed. "Yeah, you've sewn this up pretty good. But if things get desperate, you might have to try a note."

"Think things will get desperate?" Shari asked bleakly.

"Hon, with the lust of your life performing the art of dating right under your nose, I can almost guarantee it."

GENERALLY, GARRETT SPENT his Sunday evenings in solitude, locked away in his Upper East Side penthouse, dressed in old gray sweats that never saw the light of day. In full financial consultant mode, he read all his newspapers, absorbing financial reports and speculations. His clients relied on his expertise, and he enjoyed talking business with them for hours on end.

Tonight's setting was the same as always, newspapers strewn about the living room, his laptop running, a yellow legal pad and pen at the ready, Garrett seated on his plush blue sofa in the midst of it all.

But it was all just so much window dressing. Garrett was simply going through the cool and calculated motions with the fevered mind of a man obsessed.

Where was Flame?

How could he have let her get away?

Why did she want to get away?

His mystery lover, not the fluctuations of the Dow, was the focus of his scribblings tonight. Bracing his foot against the coffee table, he raised the pad to his knee again and jotted down a very exciting and seemingly inescapable conclusion, one that had been gaining shape and momentum in his mind all day long.

Maybe it was just wishful thinking on his part, but he couldn't help but lean to the idea that Flame had left the key behind on purpose, that it was all part of her plan. "If you wish to continue the game, find the door lock that matches this key." He could almost hear her whispering the taunt in his ear.

It was the explanation that made the most sense. What he and Flame had experienced was too special to dismiss so abruptly. It couldn't be the end. The key ring had to be part of her clever ruse to play on.

He tapped the pen on his angled leg, closed his eyes and let sweet memories back in. Her enchanting smile, her husky and cultured speech, her bold advances. The memory of her stretched across his body with a feline purring sound that made his blood boil.

She'd delivered him magic. It melted his reserve, gave him impetuous ideas very unbecoming to a cautious man of wealth and power. For once he was throwing caution to the wind. After years of playing it safe, dating women with all but a recorded pedigree, he was ready for a genuine, bona fide wild affair with no strings, no rules, no inhibitions.

All he needed was to locate the woman. If he ever managed to lay a hand on her again, he'd hold on a whole lot tighter.

The buzz of the door startled him. "Peters, can you get that?"

His slender, middle-aged butler appeared in the kitchen doorway, tugging his white jacket back over his shoulders for propriety's sake.

"Sorry," Garrett called out. "I suppose you were about to leave."

"That's all right, sir. I'll see to this first."

Garrett sat up straighter on the sofa cushions, anxious. "Quick, check the peephole. Is it a curvy, lusty female in her mid-twenties, boasting reams of hair with a new copper-penny shine?"

Pressing his fingers lightly against the heavy oak door, Peters squinted through the glass circle for a look. "No, sir, it's a bony female in her late fifties with a helmet of hair the shade of a buffalo nickel."

Garrett's heart sank. "Mother. Damn her timing."

"Damn mine." Peters buttoned his crisp jacket with a flourish, checking his thinning brown hair in the entry-hall mirror. "I should've been halfway back to Queens by now."

Garrett's brows rose with childish ingeniousness. "Maybe we could stay quiet, lay low. She might go away."

Peters's chest puffed, then sank with his exasperated breath. "She knows you're home on a Sunday night. You always are."

Garrett rubbed his face. "Yes, you're right. Unleash her—the door, I mean."

"Well put the first time."

Peters no sooner had the locks undone than Gwen Mc-Namara barged inside, looking smart and savvy in a teal suit. She paused to inspect him. "You look a trifle harried, Peters."

"Yes, ma'am. It's late."

"I've told you time and again it would be easier if you just boarded here round the clock."

"But my wife would miss me, ma'am."

"Oh, yes, her. Still blissfully wed then, are you?" Her nipped-and-tucked face looked pained.

"Some unions manage to elude both divorce and death for a good long time."

Gwen took the nuggets of wisdom with grace and courage. "Ah, well. Just checking."

Garrett had tossed aside his notes and was closing in quickly for the rescue. "That will do for today, Peters. See you tomorrow."

"Good night." Peters eased out the door, work jacket and all.

"Mother, I wish you'd be kinder to staff."

Gwen lingered in the entry as her son reset the locks, putting her handbag on a small antique table under the wall mirror. "In my day, staff would not have had the audacity to lead a life outside here. Not a real life, anyway. It's too distracting from duties."

"Peters is fine. I like him especially because he does have a world of his own. The last thing I need is a nursemaid—of either gender."

"But your father—"

"It's Dad who has passed on, not Mrs. Peters."

"But gracious living is something that should be encouraged in memory of your father and his father before him."

Garrett breezed back into the living room. "You'd be

hell-bent to find any employee willing to live like a monk these days. Besides, I don't care to follow Dad's style to the letter."

"But Brent was a grand success—"

"So am I."

Gwen shrugged, gliding in his wake on precariously high heels. "I see you're up to your elbows in it." She began to pick up stray sections of newspaper, murmuring something about Peters's housekeeping laxity.

Garrett quickly took up the legal pad full of personal scrawl, stuffing it under a sofa cushion when she turned her back. "Care for a sherry or something?" he asked.

She straightened, setting a stack of papers on his coffee table. "No, I don't think so. Judith St. John and I took in a matinee off-Broadway and had a long dinner at the Four Seasons. Another drink, even a small one, would put me right to sleep."

Gwen didn't look the least bit weary to Garrett. In fact, she looked radiant, expectant. Dangerous. It put him on a higher level of wariness.

"I tried to reach you on the yacht first."

"The yacht?" Garrett was taken aback. "The party's long over."

Her mouth slanted coyly. "Thought maybe you set sail again on some romantic impulse."

If only. "I have clients to see tomorrow," he protested reasonably, "solid appointments into the afternoon."

"Still, I thought this once…" She trailed off wistfully. "I hoped that perhaps some of the night's sensual wonder had rubbed off on you and you'd thrown caution to the wind."

Garrett looked at her in surprise. "There's something Dad would never have done."

"Yes, but he was married a good long time before he

reached thirty. He didn't need to be swept off his feet in a grand gesture. He had me all the while."

Visions of his father being whisked along underneath a full-size street sweeper came to Garrett's mind. He smirked, even as he felt cornered into a confession. "I hate to burst your bubble, but Flame was already on her way by sunup. The date was over and she was gone."

"Surely you didn't put her out. Or did she think she was on the clock because of the auction?" Gwen mulled the possibilities, pressing her jeweled fingers to her hollow cheeks. "A fine lady like her, forced to scurry off at the break of dawn. Disgraceful."

"You're being ridiculous," Garrett scolded, using a sudden surge of negative energy to scoop up the remaining newspapers. "Naturally we weren't measuring the date by an egg timer."

"But the high price she paid made her deserving of the finest treatment."

"I did my very best without concern for the size of her bid. Believe me, the money wasn't an issue with either of us. It was just a token, a means of getting together. And the money went to a good cause."

"You're right," Gwen said, relenting. "Anyone in our circle wouldn't think twice about the actual cost or getting her money's worth. And she is one of *us*. That kind of panache can't be faked." Worry marred her powdered face. "I just hope that she didn't feel her time was officially up, that she clearly understood your interest—"

"Cut me some slack!" His voice rose with his temper. "Knowing me as well as you do, you can imagine how awkward I felt about the whole idea of the auction in the first place. So much so that I made a point of putting it out of my mind altogether. It was a man and a woman making special magic."

Gwen surveyed his tattered sweat clothes piteously.

"I've tried over and over again to provide you with such a woman and you've always managed to trip up."

"Ah, but this lady was different from any other, truly worth getting to know, worth a little investigating."

"Then hope springs eternal!"

Garrett knew she'd been baiting him along to this end, but for once he agreed with her mission. He was a fool to ever let Flame get away.

Gwen made a gushing sound, standing on tiptoe to pinch his cheek. "Maybe I can help you reconnect with her. Whose daughter did she turn out to be?"

"That's your first thought? C'mon, I don't know who her parents are yet."

"Excuse my priorities. Who is Flame in her own right, then?"

"Ah, I don't know that, either."

Gwen snatched her hand back. "Oh, Garrett, sometimes I think you were dropped from the sky rather than sprung from my own flesh and blood."

He grinned tightly. "I think that all the time."

"Odd that she'd keep up the pretense straight through to the end, as smitten as she was." Gwen began to pace.

"I may have come up with her motives."

"All by yourself?"

He ignored her sarcasm. "Yes, I believe Flame is trying to extend the game beyond last night. I think she sneaked out on purpose with the desire to play on."

Gwen whirled, delighted. "Really. Anything to back up this theory?"

"I discovered a very significant clue aboard the yacht. I've spent the day taking steps to track her down."

"Glorious! Let me see what you found."

Garrett moved over to the rolltop desk in the corner of the room. He returned with the telling key ring. "This is my little discovery."

She snatched it up for closer scrutiny, her voice flattening. "Oh, no. Not there."

Amusement danced in his eyes. "Afraid it's true."

"I bet some member of the crew left this behind."

Garrett cleared his throat in discomfort. "No chance."

"But—"

"Take my word on that," he said firmly.

"Oh, I see…" Gwen pinkened, even her probe having some limits.

"Anyway, on the basis of this ring, I went to the Beanery to do a little investigating."

She worked her lips as though sucking on a lemon, but remained the vision of propriety. "So how are those Johnson people faring?"

Garrett overlooked her tartness, his response jovial. "Dylan and his sister, Shari, are running the place now with great success. Their patrons are upscale professionals for the most part and they're in the process of renovating the interior."

"Upscale? But this key ring is cheap plastic and metal," she protested. "Befitting the earthy Johnsons I remember."

"It's currently a fad for the customers to use the rings for their apartment keys. Harmless fun."

Gwen dropped the key ring back in his palm as though it had a smell to it. "In any case, it's difficult to imagine our Flame with one."

"Take my word for it, you're thinking of yesterday's Beanery. And there's no argument that our Flame has her playful side."

"Even if I give in on these points, how on earth do you plan to proceed?"

"Through a group that will warm your little matchmaker's heart—Club Wed."

6

"PRESSING YOUR NOSE against the front pane isn't going to bring Garrett back to the Beanery, missy."

Tracy whirled around, coming nose to nose with Shari, who was barking like an employer, smiling like a friend. "I was adding some new china saucers to the window display," she claimed. "Dylan's orders."

"That should've taken all of five minutes," Shari scoffed. Dropping her tray on a vacated table, she began to load it with dirty dishes and cutlery.

Tracy grabbed Shari's sponge to swab the table's surface. "It's only a matter of time. You know that."

"It's only Monday afternoon, a mere twenty-four hours since his last visit. And it is my problem, Trace. You know *that*." Shari seesawed her pale brows, hoisted her laded tray over her shoulder and took off.

"Oh, c'mon!" Tracy followed her behind the work station to the sinks. "This is the most exciting thing that's ever happened around here ever."

Shari set the tray down on a counter and turned with pursed lips. "That much is true."

"So quit pretending you're not turned inside out with suspense, wondering about his next move. It's only right you share the sweet agony with me."

"Sh!" Shari looked around for Dylan. Fortunately, he was too busy serving lattes to some tourists to take any notice. "I slept on this whole mess and decided to keep a clinical distance from Garrett when he returns. A clean cut emotionally is the only way."

"I've slept on it, too, and I think you're selling yourself short with this String Bean hang-up. Why not give him the chance to know the real you?"

Shari stood straight, running a hand up and down in front of her. "This is it! One dull string of a bean."

"Not exactly. There's some Flame in you, too. The girl looking for adventure, hoping to see more than the four walls of this shop."

"Even so, I wouldn't come close to fitting into the Mc-Namara mold. They use a half-dozen forks at dinner, speak snippets of twice that many foreign languages, spend money without a care."

"Well, you already know how to throw money around. That thirty thousand slipped through your fingers easily enough."

That particular sore spot made Shari visibly wince. "Surviving this invasion is all a matter of willpower. It'll be like holding a big hunk of cake in your face while you're on a diet. The taste is bound to be heavenly, but you know the consequences aren't worth it."

"Well, better get a grip on your blood sugar, 'cause guess who just came through the door!"

Garrett looked particularly tempting today, dressed in a pinstripe suit, his dark hair combed in a neat slice over his left ear.

"Walla, walla, Wall Street," Tracy crooned. "He'd need more than a fifteen-minute break to zip up here for his afternoon coffee. This smacks of real bloodhound determination."

"Yeah," Shari agreed glumly.

Dylan reached Garrett first, slapping him on the back, guiding him through the furniture cluster to the Club Wed station against the wall. Shari felt a smidgen of empathy for her brother as she read his body language. He shifted uncomfortably in his customary uniform black jeans and green T-shirt, raking a hand through his unruly blond hair and darting his eyes round the place for any clutter.

How badly Dylan wanted to match his old classmate's success. But Garrett had started with McNamara old money and made a career out of continuing in the princely tradition of investing it wisely, just like his lawyer dad. Symbolically, Dylan had been presented a bean, more in Jack-and-the-Beanstalk tradition. It would take longer to make the Johnson fortunes grow.

It was a rare occurrence for Shari to wish she could boost the morale of her annoying sibling, but in this case, she couldn't help but feel his discomfort.

"Hey, Shari!" Dylan called out. "Over here, kid."

"Come with me, Tracy," Shari urged.

"Wouldn't miss it for the world."

The pair joined the males at the Club Wed station.

"Hello, Garrett," Tracy purred. "How are finances today?"

His refined features brightened. "Fine, I guess."

"Garrett is here to stake out the place," Dylan explained needlessly. "See if he can get a line on Flame. Isn't it great, the two of us ladykillers back in business as a team, setting Manhattan on its ear?"

"Yippee." Shari smiled tightly, turning to wait on a couple of women who'd stepped up beside Dylan. They were here to pick up their Club Wed messages. Shari asked for their white membership ID cards.

"Check Garrett's file when you retrieve the messages," Dylan instructed.

"It may be a little soon," Garrett halfheartedly protested, offering his ID card.

"Not to worry," Dylan assured him. "I emptied the

mailbox myself last night and saw at least a couple addressed to you."

Shari made a beeline back to the counter with the ladies in tow and recovered a handful of square buff envelopes from the file drawer for them. They were openly pleased to have new prospects. Shari used to rejoice over the openly pleased. Now that Garrett was one of the rank and file, they only upset her. She gripped Garrett's envelopes tight. Who was nibbling at his line so soon? He wouldn't find Flame, of course, but how long would it take another prospect to replace her?

Shari was in no hurry to make Garrett's delivery. She took her time, moseying around the shop. Eventually she joined the guys at a table, where they were nursing mugs of strong brew. She hovered quietly, mesmerized by the long fingers Garrett had curled around his steaming mug. They were bound to be warmed by the ceramic and would feel so good sliding deep inside her...

"So hand 'em over, Shari," Dylan demanded anxiously.

She stared down at them dumbly, so taken up by the forbidden heat rising between her legs. "What?"

"The envelopes." Dylan finally snatched the four squares from her death grip.

Unable to leave the disaster scene, Shari scraped back a chair and sat down. She could feel Dylan's eyes drilling her in surprise, but blithely ignored him. Garrett, in the meantime, had pulled a key chain holding a small engraved penknife from his pants pocket and was methodically slitting open all four flaps.

"Hey, that's a nifty way to keep track of your keys," Dylan noted. "Too useful to lose track of."

Garrett turned the blade back into its safety catch. "It was a gift from a very important client. I'm too intimidated to lose it."

Dylan frowned. "Say, that reminds me, Shari, Tracy tells me you lost your apartment key the other day."

Propping an elbow on the table, Shari tented her fingertips along her brow, partially shielding her face. "It's no biggie. I just took a new one out of your stash upstairs."

"Fine and well. But with Garrett seated right here before you in the flesh, with a found key, it seems the perfect moment to take issue. Look how easy a girl can be traced through her key, left vulnerable to someone unscrupulous. Right, Garrett? Unscrupulous happens."

Immersed in his messages, Garrett looked up over a square of notepaper to catch only the last phrase. "You aren't calling me names, are you?"

"Just using you as an example of what could happen to Shari. If a guy with a little ingenuity had the desire to make himself a nuisance with her key, he could, quite easily."

Shari sighed, fisting her hand and setting her chin on it. "Fat chance of that."

Garrett's arresting gray eyes settled on her suddenly. "Am I missing something here?"

How can you help it, blind as a bat, thick as a plank? How excruciating that it has so little effect on your sex appeal.

"Forget the key, Dylan," she said firmly. "We'll discuss it later."

Dylan remained worried. "No, I think I'll go ahead and get a locksmith in today to change your dead bolt. Better safe than sorry. Don't you think so, Garrett?"

Garrett struggled to follow the conversation. "If her key is lost, it is better to change the lock. After all, a stranger finding your ring would automatically think it fit a door on the premises. He wouldn't necessarily know there were hundreds of them."

Dylan snapped his fingers. "Flawless logic."

"Flawless." Shari recrossed her legs and fluffed her hair with anxious energy. "So, any leads, Garrett?"

He set the notes in the center of the table. "I don't know. What do you two think?"

An open invitation for a peek. Neither Shari nor Dylan could resist.

"This Bethany 0256 is not the one," Dylan said dismissively. "She's a tiny beautician at the Rockefeller Center. And Claire 0185 is a plump redhead who works at the library down the street. Now, the other two are strangers to me. Definite possibilities...."

The men gazed at Shari. She shrugged. "I can't place the remaining two either," she admitted with some reluctance. "Maybe Tracy can eliminate them."

"I'll check. She needs service help, anyway." Dylan scooped up the notes and wended his way back to the register.

Shari and Garrett focused on the conference between the pair. Tracy ultimately shook her head and turned her attention back to the cappuccino machine.

"Guess this will take some extensive digging," he said reluctantly.

"Did you really expect her to contact you immediately?" Shari asked. "Sign off as Flame?"

"Well, yeah." His handsome face clouded. "What purpose would it serve to remain anonymous now? When I want her so badly?"

His reasoning was cunning to the point of discomfort. Shari toyed with Dylan's discarded napkin, no razor-sharp answer coming to mind. "Maybe she has her reasons," she suggested awkwardly. "Maybe she hasn't been in here to see your posting. Maybe—as I warned you before—she doesn't even belong to the Club."

"But she uses the shop key ring for her apartment key."

"For some key," she replied. "For a closet, a birdcage. Her mother's garage." Her eyes grew as he withdrew it from his pocket. He had it bad enough to carry the thing around! Had it unbelievably bad. Who'd have ever predicted she held such potency?

He turned the nail-polish-speckled disk in his hand. "Looks like an apartment key to me."

She affected a patronizing chuckle. "You're working so hard to bend every detail to your satisfaction."

"Why not? I bent to her satisfaction. Several times." He seized a breath, mortified. "Oh, damn. Sorry. That wasn't very polite."

How she hated being treated like a child. "Take it easy, Garrett," she said through gritted teeth. "As blue jokes go around here, that was pretty mild."

"I can tell you disapprove of me by the way your face is all pinched."

"Not of you. Not you." She paused, hearing the emotional catch in her voice. "The whole works is truly none of my business."

Plainly, however, she had strong opinions and they surprised and confused him. "I would think you'd be my second-best supporter after Dylan. Surely you must be hooked into the club yourself, aren't you?"

"Nope."

"Why not?"

"Mainly because Dylan would have a fit if I joined. He can't bear to think of me out on dates—"

"Because you're his baby sister."

Her blue eyes hardened. "He might tell you that, but it's mainly because I wouldn't be committing body and soul to the shop anymore if I fell for someone."

"It's probably an equal combination of the two." He paused, enjoying a pensive moment. "You really were half the team's baby sister, you know. Seeing you again this way, so cute and spunky, I find myself still tempted to join in on the guiding and teasing.''

She clasped her hands together with a joyful coo. "Ah, another brother. Just what I need!"

He chuckled, raising a palm in surrender. "Okay, so you're not thrilled. But there should never be a penalty for fond nostalgia.''

Behind her sweet smile Shari opted for the death penalty.

Garrett shuffled through the two accounted-for notes, feeling a trifle awkward. "So, how do people generally handle the initial contact?''

"It's customary to meet right here," she reported dutifully. "That's part of the lure of the club, one-stop shopping and courting. For the price of a cup of coffee, two people can look each other over on neutral and familiar territory, make firmer plans for intimacy only if it feels right.''

"Sounds pleasant enough.''

"Sure." Her gaze strayed, her voice lifted airily. "Unless you happen to be looking for a needle in a haystack.''

"Cut that out!''

"What, Garrett?''

"Being argumentative with no just cause." He reached across the table to tweak her cheek, his voice dipping to a growl. "Like it or not, you're still the busy little String Bean, stirring things up, making guys crazy.''

Funny, he hadn't noticed anything of the kind when he had his hands all over her, Shari thought ironically. "Garrett," she said in clear exasperation, "I'm a grown woman.''

"So you're causing havoc in automatic pilot then, completely unaware.''

Ha! Shari was totally aware—especially of the shaky

territory they were treading on. She could almost feel the floor tremble beneath her chair. Too strong a protest over his search might get him thinking things over, the gooey way she'd originally greeted him, the way she'd lost her key, her stupid crack earlier on about the thirty-grand club fee. He just might let his mind wander, begin to imagine what she'd look like with some hair tint and makeup, suspect there were some curves beneath her baggy denims.

"Guess I'll leave messages for these two," Garrett ultimately decided.

"Well, you know where the stationery is," she said with forced gaiety.

Without further ceremony, he scrambled toward the Club Wed station.

"YOU SHOULD BE GLAD Garrett's decided to meet prospective Flames here." Tracy couldn't resist making the comment to Shari a week later as Garrett ordered two lemon-lime Italian sodas for his table in the back. "If he gave each one the lavish dinner-and-dancing treatment, it would greatly increase the odds of him falling into an unexpected romance."

"True." Shari sighed, wrapping the last of the freshly made sandwiches in cellophane. Still, as predicted, it was awful to be in the vicinity of his fruitless search. Tracy never let her slice anything while he was on the premises, fearful she'd sink her knife into something essential while she pretended not to watch one mating ritual after another. There were so many prospective mates—at least four a day—that he'd begun to bring his cell phone and laptop, curb his caffeine intake with non-coffee choices.

Naturally, Flame was never among the candidates. And according to Dylan, never once did Garrett arrange to meet a woman for something more meaningful. Shari was flattered and disturbed. But where would it all end? His anticipation was so tangible she could almost touch it.

How badly she wanted to touch every inch of his anticipation...

"Oh, by the way," Tracy sang out as she prepared to take flight with a tray laden with lattes and pastries, "the interior decorator Dylan lined up is coming in this afternoon for a consultation."

Shari stared at her blankly. "What's the rush?"

"Dylan set this up a long time ago, remember?"

"Yeah, back in the days when I had a fat inheritance to pay for it."

"He wants you to take the quote, decide if it's reasonable."

Her soft brow furrowed. "I happen to be in a very unreasonable mood."

Tracy shifted her tray from one arm to another, tossing her mane of lush raven hair over her shoulder. "What will that get you but a little time?"

Shari squeezed her friend's arm. "Oh, Tracy, I feel like this whole place is on the verge of explosion because of Garrett's desperate energy. If that happens, it won't matter whether the Formica is a cracked old pumpkin color or pearl-white Corian, right?"

"Shari, as much as Dylan can be a tyrant, he deserves the truth, some forewarning that his remodeling plans will soon be hitting a snag."

"I won't have to face him for hours yet. He took off early to run some errands, then he'll be at the dentist half the afternoon having that crown fitted."

"But he will be back, deserving answers."

"Don't give me that accusing look. I'm not ready to fess up."

"You will have to eventually."

"After Garrett tires of his search, I'll find a way to explain everything to Dylan. In the meantime, I plan to stall on the improvements."

Tracy turned Shari's attention to Garrett's table, where he sat with a bouncy little brunette who was chattering a mile a minute. "How ironic that Mr. Finance is the ultimate cash source and the very reason you're tapped out."

Shari's mind drifted from financial ruin and irony to sympathetic amusement. There was a glazed look in Garrett's gray eyes that she recalled from their school days, specifically their ballroom-dance-lesson days in Lily Fleur's bright, airy, second-floor loft. His mother, Gwen, had insisted he take the lessons his freshman year in preparation for future functions, and Garrett, in turn, had insisted that Dylan be treated to the same. Dylan, frequently saddled with the job of looking after Shari during shop hours, had taken her along. Because they often needed an extra female partner, Shari, too, had benefited from the lessons and was often coupled with Garrett, learning every move in the same exact rhythm and manner.

Did he ever stop to wonder why she'd been so fluid in his arms on the yacht?

On the yacht... No matter how many times she repeated the phrase, it lost none of its sparkle. Garrett was such a glorious catch, equipped with all the extras. Lucky the woman who could satisfy fussy, uppercrust Gwen McNamara. With a jab of relief Shari knew it wouldn't be this bouncy brunette. She had a nose ring and a hyena laugh. Hardly McNamara material. Even now, the girl was rising ever so reluctantly from her chair, allowing Garrett to give her hand a perfunctory pump of farewell.

Shari grabbed an empty tray and swooped down on his table. "Ah, another dead end, I see."

"Right on."

She set the tray on the table. Garrett, so accustomed to the drill, placed the empty glasses on it. "We also carry some bottled juices if you're tired of coffee and soda," she told him.

"Wipe that smirk off your face."

"Excuse me?"

"You know, that master-of-lost-causes smirk."

She clucked in regret, sliding into the chair opposite. "I'm afraid it might be permanent now, frozen in place so long."

"Well, do you have any fresh suggestions?"

Her sigh was deep and heartfelt. "Not really."

"What would you do in my place, after spending the night of my life with the perfect lover?"

"That's a tough question."

"See!"

"But I do have an answer."

"Of course."

She leaned over, gripping the edges of the tray. "I would ground myself in reality, first of all. Accept that one night was just a fantasy brought to life."

"But—"

"You are looking for a spouse, aren't you?"

"Probably."

"Garrett, dabbling in Club Wed is a two-way street. The women you're parading in here are looking for genuine commitment."

Staring into her vivid blue eyes, Garrett could feel his innermost feelings being torn out of his gut, up through his throat. Telling her things had always been so easy. In part she'd been a good listener because she was too young to fully understand. What was his excuse now?

The same, he wanted to think. She still seemed so untouched, so charmingly innocent.

"I don't mean to lead anybody on," he assured her. "But I have no other way of searching for Flame. And I do have clear intentions of settling down with her if everything clicks. Though marriage with her would never be described as settling down, I'm sure."

"But what if matrimony wasn't on her mind? What if she just wanted a crazy fling?"

"In that case, I'm gambling that with a little coaxing she could want more."

"Don't you think a man should focus on a more realistic kind of woman for his lifetime mate? Someone to raise his children? Comfort him through the rough times?"

He was stunned by her fervor. "What are you suggesting?"

That you get the hell out of here and stop torturing me with past memories and visions of a hopeless future. "It's not up to me to tell you what to do," she squawked.

"Why do I get the feeling that you'd like to do exactly that?"

She waved her hand. "Maybe it's because I'm accustomed to running the club, listening to members' troubles. I guess I have a wealth of experience and it shows."

"That's not experience."

"Sure it is."

"There's a vast difference between eavesdropping and living. We'll talk again when you get a love life of your own." He stood in a huff, gathering up his laptop and cell phone and stuffing them into his briefcase.

"Why, you arrogant ass!"

To her surprise he chuckled. "I have to go."

She popped out of the chair. "Oh? Insulted beyond repair?"

"No, I have a consultation. But I'll be back around four to meet Jena 1689."

"WHERE DID YOU SAY your offices are, Garrett?"

"Wall Street."

"Am I boring you?"

Garrett mustered a smile for the woman seated opposite him. She was dressed in orange leggings and a sweater, and her shaggy brown hair was streaked with white. Jena 1689. Straight out of the Addams Family album with her offbeat poetry, piercing eyes and flour-white complexion.

"Sorry," he murmured politely, "I was just thinking of some...unfinished business." That business happened to be getting the best of Shari Johnson and her snappy retorts. At the moment she was bustling around the coffee shop with Dylan's remodeling sketch in her hands, a pompous decorator named Kyle Saunders at her side taking notes, offering suggestions.

"The corporate jungle will kill you in the end," Jena cautioned. "Hold it! I feel an inspirational ditty coming on." She rummaged through the knapsack on the empty chair beside her for a pen, then began to scribble on a paper napkin at a furious pace, chanting aloud. "Jungle, jungle, I live for thee. Jungle of cash, I kneel to thee. Jungle have an exit, set me free." Triumphant with her handiwork, she pushed the napkin across the table. "Here, this is for you. Something to keep in case I hit the big time."

"Gee. Thanks."

She leaned back to autograph the ditty. "There! I like to leave my mark on everything. Just in case I'm ever discovered."

Garrett's smile was strained. "Unpredictable things do happen."

"If I hit the big time, you could donate that napkin to some worthy cause—say, for the environment. They could sell it for big money to fund research, and we'd all benefit from that research. So goes the circle of life."

Why did Shari wear such baggy clothes all the time? he fleetingly wondered. Her Beanery T-shirts were consistently at least a size too large. He tried to imagine what she'd look like in a smaller one, tucked into her jeans....

"If that isn't enough to rock you," Jena confided excitedly, "I've been considering setting my stuff to music."

He reinstated eye contact with his guest. "Oh?"

"Folk songs with a rap beat. Say, are you trying to catch that waitress's attention? I mean, you spend half your time craning in your chair, keeping track of her moves."

Caught in the act of ogling Dylan's kid sister when he thought he was being so subtle. He couldn't possibly come up with a logical explanation that would satisfy even himself. What he did know was that bit by bit, Shari was getting a hold on him in a most disturbing way. Had she always been this irritating? This interesting? This quick on the verbal draw?

"I think I recognize that man she's just showing out," he blurted out lamely. "He's a decorator from Elite House. My parents used him for a guest cottage once."

She was horrified. "It would be a shame to change this place."

"Things wear out. Need to be replaced. It happens."

"My aunt had a hip replaced and started seeing visions of aliens."

Something inside Garrett snapped then. He tried to be kind with every mismatch, but this folk-rapper was the limit. He drained his lukewarm coffee in a gulp. "I don't mean to be rude, Jena," he said with resolve, "but I feel it would be unfair to both of us to continue meeting."

"Oh?" Jena was startled.

"We have nothing in common," he reasoned. "Not that it hasn't been nice meeting you, of course."

"Yeah, sure." She rose to her feet, hoisting her knapsack over her bony shoulder. A flint of pride hardened her eyes. "Guess you're right. If I had felt something, I would've defied the management ages ago by slipping you some dried-apple chips underneath the table."

He rose, too. "Well, that dehydrated stuff will no doubt keep for Mr. Right," he said helpfully. "Has an incredible shelf life."

"I'm sure," she said tartly. "Goodbye."

Garrett shifted from one foot to another with a grimace. Shari had to be getting the biggest kick out of Jena, especially as it was mere hours after they'd had their spirited little chat about his mission and her inexperience. It would be easy enough to slip out of the shop at this point. He didn't even have his briefcase to weigh him down anymore. Oddly, the fact that she didn't seem to be paying him any mind at the moment took all the fun out of an escape. Rather than leave his money on the table, he strolled up to the cash register.

"Hey."

Shari's head snapped up from the yellow form she had spread out on the counter between a napkin holder and a sugar bowl. "Oh. You still here?"

"Of course!"

"Your choice, I guess." With a shrug she returned to the sheet.

"Aren't you going to break into some folk-rap drivel about the jungle, too?"

"Huh?" She pushed her specs up her nose to survey him closer.

"C'mon, don't be shy."

"Don't be stupid," she blustered in return.

Garrett gave her his guest check and a twenty-dollar bill. She mutely rang it up.

"What's with you?" he demanded. "This last woman was a prime example of how fruitless my search is, a figure you should be having great fun with."

Shari exhaled, releasing a heavy burden. "Sorry. I was just going over this estimate from Elite House, and is it ever steep."

"They are an upscale design firm."

"I know. Dylan's first choice. He wants the best of everything."

"The best is bound to be pricey."

She was clearly exasperated. "Look, Garrett, I want us to have quality. But—but I'd like to get a value for my dollar, too."

"Elite has a fine reputation." He lowered his voice. "And according to Dylan, you both agreed to pump your inheritance from Aunt Lucille into this project. Sounds like it should cover things quite nicely."

All that money gone forever but still buying her endless torture at the mercy of this man. Resting her elbows on the counter, she rubbed her forehead. "Sometimes life can get tricky when you don't have a limitless well of the stuff."

The remark was meant to sting, and it hit Garrett off guard. Did his wealth upset Shari? Probably. He sensed that everything about him caused her endless static.

"But we will manage," she went on to assure him. "I am responsible for this phase of the project and I'll come through. It just may not be Elite...."

Dylan strolled through the entrance moments later, his cheek slightly swollen from his trip to the dentist.

"Hey, no chipmunks allowed!" Shari gibed cheerily,

grateful for the distraction. Garrett was set to probe into her money matters like a terrier sniffing out a bone. She supposed it was a habit of an investment consultant to poke into other people's finances, to try to assist them. Unfortunately, it was the last thing she wished to discuss in this lifetime. With a sleight of hand she pulled Kyle Saunders's outrageous bid sheet off the counter, folded it and stuck it in her pocket.

"Any wuck wid taday's bash?" Dylan asked, his speech obviously slurred by an injection of painkiller.

In Garrett's disgusted mood, it was fairly easy to keep a straight face over Dylan's Donald Duck voice. "No luck with today's batch, and I'm finished with this appointment marathon. The whole process is so disappointing. The minute these ladies walk through the door it's clear none of them are my Flame. Still, I'm forced to go through the amenities, wasting their time—and mine. This could go on forever, and I don't have the stamina."

Dylan scowled, stroking his swollen cheek. "We need a pwan B."

"I'm not so sure there is one."

The men bickered a little about Garrett's surrender. Then, in a bumbling way, Dylan invited Garrett to the Thursday-night basketball workout at the YMCA, an informal group made up of their old Brady High team. "I suppose you already have plans for tonight. It is short notice."

"I'd love to come. Sure there's a spot for me?"

Dylan was taken aback by his enthusiasm. "Naturally."

Shari tensed. Good grief. Now on top of everything else, Garrett was going to join those bums down at the Y every week. At this rate of bonding, the Beanery would soon be his second home! She couldn't bear the cycle much longer, watching him yearn for his dream lover while she yearned for him. If only she could put a complete stop to his infatuation. He was halfway there, giving up his appointments. Fueled by a mission, Shari marched to the back of the shop where Tracy was filling sugar jars on a stainless steel table.

"I'm taking your advice."

"I don't follow," Tracy said distractedly, driving a plastic scoop into a giant sugar bag.

"About leaving Garrett a kiss-off note from Flame."

"No kidding." She turned to face Shari with interest. "Why now?"

"Because he's weakening. The chase is getting to him and he's finished with appointments. If ever there was an opening for Flame to give him the heave-ho, this is it."

Tracy thought this over while she poured sugar into the last empty jar. "Don't forget about Dylan. He's having the time of his life with Garrett's infatuation. He'll continue to do all he can to keep it alive, twist any note to his advantage. After all, it will be just the proof he needs that Flame is indeed a customer."

"Dylan has tomorrow off, though," Shari reminded her, moving closer to tighten the lids on the full jars. "Envision Garrett getting a call from, say, you, Tracy, about a buff envelope addressed to him. We get him over here, watch him open it and back up his decision to take Flame's brush-off as the final frustration."

"Worth a shot."

"So will you help me write the note?"

"With pleasure." Excitement danced in Tracy's eyes. "We'll make it a real heart tugger. A Danielle Steele masterpiece!"

7

"BELIEVE ME, GARRETT, Shari won't mind. I bring the
guys here all the time after B-ball. At least twice a
month."

Dylan's casual assurances struck Garrett as rather
thoughtless, but the ragtag bunch of his old classmates
jamming the hallway above the Beanery seemed completely at ease, even anxious to crash Shari's apartment.

"It's after ten-thirty—"

"It always is. She knows we don't get the court until
eight."

Garrett shifted the case of beer he was carrying from
his right hand to his left, aiming a thumb at the door
across the hallway that he'd entered a thousand times
years back. "Aren't you living right over there, in your
folks' old apartment?"

Dylan lifted the plastic sack from the video rental
place. "Yeah, but I don't have a wide-screen TV or a decent VCR. Not to mention food in the fridge. I live on the
shop's leftovers." Dylan laid a heavy fist on his sister's
door.

Locks tripped, the door creaked open. Shari peered
out. Confronted with the half-dozen jocks fresh out of
the shower with slicked-back hair, clinging sweats and
lopsided grins, she gasped in horror. "You were here
just last week!"

"So you're busy?" Dylan asked doubtfully.

"In my own way," she retorted. Shari had never reacted this coolly to Dylan's friends before, so she understood the surprise on their faces. But seeing Garrett's sinfully handsome face among the bunch was enough to throw her for a loop. She knew he'd joined tonight's casual scrimmage but hadn't counted on the guys coming back here on a consecutive Thursday, something they'd never done before. They were still high school boys at heart, however—boastful, boisterous, selfish. She should have learned ages ago to expect the unexpected from them.

Dylan was tapping his track shoe on the scuffed tiles as she did a body block in the doorjamb. "What are you doing in there that's so private? Some kind of lab experiment?"

"I'm cooking."

He leaned closer, sniffing appreciatively. "What a coincidence, we're starving. Is that Italian by any chance?"

"Lasagna—"

He clapped her cheeks. "Ah, I could kiss you. We all could!"

A hearty roar of approval took Shari aback, allowing a narrow path for the guys. They took advantage by barging inside, tugging her ponytail and nudging her shoulder.

A minuscule figure in the throng of muscle, she shouted out a weak protest. "But—but I was planning to freeze it for my own personal dinners."

"It's a compliment that we love your chow," Dylan insisted, pausing to admire the new dead bolt he'd had installed earlier in the day. "Remember, babe," he said, shoving the door into place, "gotta keep this locked. Especially when you're alone."

"Yeah, yeah." Shari made a hissing sound between her teeth. "Hey! No feet on my coffee table, Jimbo. Your wife doesn't allow that at home—I asked her!"

Garrett handed off the case of beer to Mark, who in turn ambled for the kitchenette on the right. Garrett rocked on his heels, feeling slightly awkward in the melee, unaccustomed to imposing on anyone so obviously reluctant. But the evening had been a grand hit so far; it felt super being one of the rowdy guys again, indulging in friendship for the sake of simple pleasure rather than for a host of ulterior motives. On some planes Dylan seemed as surface and simple as yesterday, but on others he was remarkably astute.

For instance, Dylan sure said it straight when he pegged Shari as downright kissable. She was radiant in a pale pink T-shirt and short shorts of a rosier hue, her pale hair gathered up in a bouncy ponytail. The image mingled girlish remembrances and womanly promise in a neat little package that confused and aroused him.

If it weren't for Flame's brand on him, who knew...

Still, there was no denying the subtle chemistry growing between them with each verbal skirmish. A strange phenomenon, considering that he'd always felt in the driver's seat with Shari, one giant step ahead of her. Things had changed along the way; clearly, a man could easily become putty in her hands. But he was already putty in Flame's hands. He couldn't fret over two women at the same time. Could he?

Garrett came back to reality as he heard Dylan talking about putty. He was in the process of pinching his sister's cheek.

"Okay, so maybe putty isn't a fair color comparison," Dylan conceded. "But your complexion is paler than usual. I wouldn't like to see heavy makeup on you, but the usual dash of blush and lipstick were nice."

"Stop playing warden."

He was startled by her murderous glare. "Okay, okay."

Suddenly feeling Garrett's eyes upon her, Shari pinkened naturally. She'd given up all makeup for fear that something might trip in Garrett's brain, give cause to link her to Flame. If he didn't hang around the shop so much, she could go back to being herself, with moderate flair and color.

But what sensitive female could ever turn out a man so handsome, so admiring? One sensitive enough to realize when a lady would have rather kept her lasagna all to herself? His genuine discomfort and appreciative eye easily made up for his cracks about her inexperience earlier in the day.

Mark Plant popped his curly red head out of her cramped kitchen, poised for complaint. "I want you guys to know that the lasagna isn't put together. The sauce is on the stove, the noodles are in the sink and the cheese is on the counter."

"Don't just stand there, stir that sauce," Shari called out over the chorus of groans. "And turn off the burner."

As usual, Dylan insisted upon playing host in his sister's place, turning on lamps and her television. But Shari had to admit he seemed to be taking the chow delay with uncharacteristic patience. "Why don't you guys pop a movie in the VCR and crack open some beers," he suggested, backing toward the door. "I have to run down to the shop for a minute."

Dylan left quickly. Shari watched the guys settle into her cramped living room, then with a sigh went back to the kitchen to cook.

Garrett sat down on a cushioned footstool that matched Jim Travis's chair and tried to watch the Sly Stallone flick with enthusiasm, cheering at random acts of violence between gulps of beer. But all the while he was torn between the gender lines. Didn't any of them care that Shari was putting together a meal for them at this hour?

Waiting until the guys were too engrossed in the movie to harass him, Garrett eased into the kitchen. "Need any help?"

Shari had just slipped her pan of lasagna into the oven. She closed the door with a thump and whirled around. "Oh! You startled me."

"Sorry."

She rolled her eyes, but there was a trace of humor in their blue depths. "It's just that no one ever crosses the line during the preparations."

"Lines are made to be crossed." He sauntered closer. Close enough to catch a trace of her fruity shampoo, for his bare forearm to graze hers. As the electric current traveled his spine, he was glad he had, at the coaxing of his pals, hacked off the sleeves of his Ralph Lauren sweatshirt. "I can help out, if you like."

She gestured to the table, already stacked with plates and forks. "Not much to do anymore. Though you could check my freezer to see if there's a loaf of garlic bread among the ice-cube trays."

He continued to hover, glancing down into the vee of her tight knit top. Dylan had been mistaken about her pallor. Why, every time he was within her range these days she got pink in a hurry, a pink that traveled down her throat to her small breasts, currently on lush display in a pushup bra.

Shari happened to be one of those women who didn't need a lot of war paint. Would he be disappointed when Flame removed hers?

Shari felt a small tremor of longing as he openly admired her. Common sense cautioned her body not to respond. This man had a lot of nerve, considering he was hooked on someone else. Even if she was the other

woman, too, it was no excuse for this blatant come-on.
For all he knew, he was focusing on two entirely different women at once!

"The freezer's inside that big humming box," she
murmured, gesturing to the compact refrigerator
wedged between the sink and the wall. "And that
bread's not getting any younger."

"Right!" Garrett abruptly took the three necessary
steps across the room, tugging open the freezer door and
reaching his hand inside to shift icy packages around.
His hand wasn't the only piece of him that needed to be
cooled off. If it were a chest freezer, he'd be tempted to
climb inside for a nice long chilling out.

Shari shouldn't be getting to him this way. Not the
String Bean, who'd witnessed countless events in his
clumsy adolescence: the name of every girl he'd ever
dated or tried to date, the times his parents barged into
the Johnsons' coffee shop to drag him off to some cul-
tural event or lesson, his attempts to roughen up his designer threads just to appear worthily scruffy—as he had
tonight with the hacked sleeves. All those vulnerabili-
ties—and more—best forgotten.

With Flame, he had a clean slate, appeared the rich
and invincible financier without a single weakness. This
was in direct counterpoint to the little-sister type who
lived with one eye trained on the rearview mirror, col-
lecting awkward memories for future capitalization.

So was that what it had come to? Comparing the subtle, pleasingly ordinary Shari with his reckless siren from
the bachelor auction?

This was crazy. He'd gone years without feeling anything deep for a woman. Now he'd snagged two at once!
The odds seemed highly unlikely, but there was no getting around it.

"So, Garrett, that hand frozen yet?" Shari taunted.

Garrett stiffened with awareness, feeling like a damn fool standing at the open freezer like a dope. With a start he discovered those plain blue eyes of hers were suddenly all aglitter in a very sharp, observant way. Damned if she still didn't have the capacity to read him like a storybook. Most likely she was only getting half the story, though. By the prickly edge to her tone, she probably figured he was putting a strain on her refrigerator thinking exclusively of Flame.

What would she do if she knew the truth about his torn desires? Calmly laugh it off, probably, let him down easy. After all, in sheer self-defense, she'd learned to manipulate Dylan by humoring him. That same attitude would apply to all his buddies, too.

Maybe he wasn't falling for Shari, but rather was envious of the way she still tolerated her big brother's attempts to show her guidance and affection. An only child, Garrett could only imagine a bond so complex and tight. Maybe he still wished for siblings on some level.

No, that wasn't true. Those yearnings had never been strong enough even years ago to explain away his attraction to Shari now. She was simply wonderful, worth knowing. And deserving of a completely devoted suitor, he reminded himself, not some guy passing through, already distracted by a sexy siren.

"Hey, Mr. Freeze!" Shari snatched the bread out of the freezer and smacked it on the countertop. "You ever hear of gangrene?"

Garrett pushed the freezer door closed, rubbing his cold hand. "I'm degrees from that."

"You're so busy thinking about Flame, I could've stuck your head in there without a struggle."

So she did know, and she cared. It fueled his courage, loosened his tongue. "I was thinking more about you," he insisted softly.

"Me?" She was genuinely aghast.

But not displeased, he noted, moving into her space, trapping her between the counter and his body. "Yes, how you deserve an open and honest relationship with just the right guy."

Who? Him? Shari wondered, taken aback. He could never see her in his future, surely. As for Mother Gwen, she found Shari dead common. He had to be goofing around.

Still, it was difficult not to respond with real emotion. His eyes were blazing down on her now, sparkling silver, full of curiosity and promise, holding a gentleness that he hadn't revealed to Flame. Shari could feel a meltdown in her thighs, spreading fast to other places, making lucid thought unlikely. Good thing she'd already decided days ago that she should never risk kissing him again. He might taste Flame in her mouth.

All that garlic she'd chopped for her pasta dish—if only she'd chewed on some when she had the chance. That would have kept him clear!

His hand curved her chin, tipped her face up. Memories of earlier kisses with her alter ego flashed to mind, made her shiver in anticipation. It would be best to stand her ground now, though. She definitely wouldn't kiss him.

But what if he did the honors? As his firm mouth covered hers with a familiar enticing warmth, she decided that small technicality would be enough to justify her response.

His kiss was tentative, only to gradually deepen as she rested her hands on his chest. It took all her self-control not to boldly match his strokes, brand him as Flame had. But the risk was way too high. Maybe with time he might come to forget how her alter ego tasted, behaved.

But for now the memories were all too fresh and intoxicating.

Did he suspect? Not yet, it seemed. Her pale lashes had fluttered open to watch him. He was relaxed, savoring what he thought was new and uncharted territory. Caution called to her from the far corners of her mind to stop now before she couldn't stop.

"Hey, where's Garrett?" Dylan's abrupt boom and door slam marked his return to the apartment. And seemed just the welcome excuse Shari needed for a huddle break. She gave Garrett a shove that set him back six inches or so. Not the mile she'd have preferred, but certainly enough to bewilder her emotionally dense brother. Dylan never could quite see her as a woman with sexual needs and would, for his own peace of mind, gladly overlook any incriminating body language.

"You'll never guess what." Dylan rushed into the cramped kitchen.

Shari gulped. It wasn't a tough mystery—as Dylan was clutching a single cream-colored envelope. Damn, it had to be Garrett's only Club Wed message of the day, Flame's buzz-off letter! She'd forgotten all about it in the heat of the moment. And what a fool trick to bring it up now.

Garrett appeared no happier. "I hope that isn't a note for me, Dylan. I've given up the club. You took my card down from the board yourself."

Dylan looked about to burst with excitement as he slapped the envelope in his friend's hand. "I couldn't help checking, it's become such a fun habit." Torn between his Cupid duties and his hunger, he sniffed the fragrant air, then nudged between the couple, snatching up the foil sack of bread from the counter and sliding it in the oven beside the lasagna. "Let's check it out before we eat."

"Maybe he'd rather read the note in private," Shari suggested.

Dylan thumped the oven door closed. "Aw, never has before."

Garrett looked pained but extracted a knife from her butcher block on the counter. With a quick slice he opened the envelope.

As he tugged the note free of its cover, Shari bit her lip painfully hard. Her plan to spoon-feed this message to Garrett herself was a bust. Dylan was primed to come on strong, influence Garrett with peer pressure. And to make matters worse, Garrett was bound to be embarrassed in front of the guys, as well. No fun as a teenager or adult.

"It's from her," Dylan reported excitedly, glancing at the note without a qualm—or permission, for that matter. "I can see the signature at the bottom clearly."

Garrett backed into the door of the broom closet in an effort to absorb his message in private. His expression was inscrutable. "Guess it's over."

"What do you mean?" Dylan snatched the paper away, reading it aloud. Shari read along for appearances' sake, even though she knew it by heart. It had taken the women an hour to compose it.

"Dear Garrett,
How flattering that you are searching for me! I truly cherish our time spent together, but feel our passion was meant to burn just for the night. After all, real love in real life is never so whimsical or perfect. Since we could not hope to sustain such pleasure, why not just hold tight to our flawless memory?
                              Best of luck in the future, Flame"

Dylan returned the note to Garrett, awestruck. "You know what this means, don't you?"

"She's dumped me for a second time," Garrett said flatly.

"No! Well, yes."

Garrett, unaccustomed to expressing so much emotion—first with Shari, now with Flame—struggled for balance. "I'm a practical man, Dylan. Maybe this is just the closure I need."

"No way, not with these fresh clues to go on."

"She isn't baiting me, she's dumping me."

"But this development should whet your appetite. Flame has been in our humble establishment—is definitely a member of Club Wed. She has actually walked among us and we didn't know it." Dylan swiveled on his athletic shoes to confront Shari. "So, little sister, what did you see tonight?"

Shari cringed as a hush fell over the kitchen. "I didn't see anyone put a note in the box tonight. And that's the plain truth."

"Was Tracy there?"

Shari thought fast to remove her friend from the inquisition. "She checked the box before she punched out and it was empty."

"Jeeze." Dylan's strong jaw sagged like a boy denied ice cream. "If only it hadn't been a Thursday night, I would've been around."

Shari patted her brother's back, unable to completely hide her cynicism for his meddling. "Tough break, Cupid."

Dylan stared at Garrett in wonder. "I can't believe this is the end. It's so hard to imagine a woman not wanting a second crack at you."

Garrett knew it was supposed to be a compliment, but all he heard was what he thought Shari was hearing, that perhaps he hadn't satisfied his lover. Just like the old days she was bearing witness to the doubts, the insecurities.

"She said right there in the note that she had a great time," he replied defensively.

"Seems more likely that she's just playing hard to get 'cause she knows you like it that way," Dylan asserted triumphantly, waving to his pals to join him in a chorus of support. "The same old Garrett, wanting what he can't have."

"That may be part of it." Garrett broke off self-consciously, avoiding Shari's belligerent stare. He'd been trying to sort out that very question himself lately. Did he want Flame back just because she was playing so hard to get? Or was the woman behind the illusion worthy of his chase? In his own defense, she had seemed so genuinely right for him that night.

Hearing the quandary voiced aloud by Dylan humbled him. Garrett knew the image the others had always had of him held a great deal of truth: given everything he desired since his toddler days had made him all the more intrigued with things just out of reach. Was it the passion of the chase he enjoyed, or the passions of Flame herself?

"C'mon, Garrett," Dylan urged. "Give me the word that this hunt isn't over just yet."

The last thing Garrett wanted to do was insult Shari with his attraction to Flame. But it wouldn't be fair to lead her on until he could get Flame out of his system, would it? "Maybe it would be a good thing to at least speak to Flame—at least for some kind of closure."

"That's the spirit!" Dylan rejoiced, edging by Shari to clamp an arm around his pal's shoulders.

Shari stumbled into the hallway, forgotten as the males embellished this new development with schoolboy zeal. She'd taken a gamble and lost. With the guys' help, Garrett had come to accept that he'd been attracted to Flame in the first place because she presented a challenge. Now he was going to hold out for another meeting for that same reason. Things would be worse than ever now, with the confirmation that Flame was indeed a patron of the Beanery. True, Garrett didn't seem quite as ecstatic about it as Dylan did, but he'd all but dumped her again in favor of her alter ego. How could he after the sweet kiss they'd just shared?

Shari was both empowered and frustrated by the fact that she could have made that kiss far more memorable, left him a mound of gelatin if she'd tried.

Maybe she should have tried. Thrown caution to the wind. Really given Garrett McNamara something to stew about!

The hurrah around Garrett continued until the oven timer pinged. Changing his priority to the feast ahead, Dylan tugged Shari back into the fray. The hungry crowd parted before her, allowing a clear path to the oven.

"Say, I forgot to ask you how it went with Kyle Saunders, sis. He go for my remodeling sketches?"

Dylan would rake up her other weakness, the spend-thrift purchase! She snapped off the timer and the stove, weighing a short, dismissive reply. "He was impressed. Liked the hunter-green-and-brass scheme."

"Something he can do, then?"

"I guess," she said cautiously.

"Great. So you made the arrangements?"

"Not yet." Shari took a deep breath. "You see, I found his estimate rather high."

"But you have forty grand and some change," Dylan argued.

She plucked oven mitts from hooks on the wall. Clapping them together, she wished they were boxing gloves.

How she'd like to pop some nosy male nose. "Still, I should have some say about how much of it I intend to sink in the remodeling."

"I'm willing to put my share into the new plumbing and wiring and half the appliances," he argued.

"I know. But I keep seeing my future as broader than the scope of the shop. I believe it might be in my best interest to invest some of my money in something else."

"That's childish hogwash! The folks were content with running the place."

Her eyes slanted toward the group of dispersing jocks. They were well accustomed to the Johnson siblings' fireworks and found it a dull display at best. But Garrett looked both shell-shocked and entranced. She speculated that he wasn't accustomed to such blunt confrontation, being an only child with restrained parents. And the fact they were bickering about money probably only heightened the financial adviser's curiosity.

So many clues were swirling around him, connecting Shari to Flame. At the rate he was absorbing information, there was an increasing possibility that he might stumble upon the truth.

"Dylan, this probably isn't the best time for a quarrel," she stated firmly. "I intend to shop around a little for the best deal, end of story."

Dylan clamped a hand to his forehead. "I'm not sure I'm even hungry anymore."

"You are. You always are." Shari smacked the quilted mitts into his hands. "Here. Have a ball."

"Where are you going?"

"Over to your place for some peace. Good night!"

GARRETT WAS WALKING his treadmill early Sunday afternoon when he noticed the door to his penthouse study opening. It was Peters, of course, standing on the doorsill in his crisp white butler's jacket. Garrett pried the headphones, streaming with the Rolling Stones, off his ears and gave Peters his full attention.

"I thought I'd head out now, sir, if you don't mind."

"Sure, go ahead."

Peters paused in half swing. "Oh, by the way, you have a caller—"

"Surprise!" Before the butler could finish his droll announcement, Gwen breezed by him into the study.

Garrett was surprised but managed a smile as Gwen closed in on him. He slowed his pace on the conveyor belt. "I thought Peters had someone on the phone."

"Thought maybe we could catch a show. Even a movie would be nice."

"Where are all your ladies?" he blurted out in mild complaint.

"Everyone who matters is tied up today. Could have spent a quiet afternoon, I suppose, but then I thought of you, wondered if you might be lonely."

Spending time around the blunt Johnson clan gave him the inspiration to let down his emotional guard a fraction and chip some of hers. With determination he switched off his music and the treadmill motor. Hopping off the belt, he exchanged his headphones for the towel on his rolltop desk. His expression was tender as he mopped his face and advanced on her.

"Why are you looking at me like that?" she demanded briskly.

He regarded her patiently. "Mother, you don't have to pretend. I know you especially miss Dad on Sundays. No matter how busy his schedule, he set aside that day for you. It's all right to want to fill those hours. They have to be lonelier than the rest."

"How dare you psychoanalyze me? The very idea..."

She stiffened and turned away, reminding Garrett of an icicle in her pale blue shirtwaist dress.

"I'm being an observant son, that's all."

"We lose, we grieve, we go on. It's expected."

Garrett took her arm and turned her back to him. "That's a fine front for the outside world, but appearances shouldn't matter as much between us."

She gasped. "Appearances always matter."

"But we're a family."

She shook her silvery bob with force. "Your point is lost on me."

Garrett pressed on anyway. "We should be able to let down our guard at times."

"Restraint is a necessity in all matters," she asserted coldly. "Do you really think the family fortunes would've sailed steadily if we hadn't been in control during the hours after Brent's heart attack?"

"That's fine for the public—"

"It's all the same, son, a rock-solid stand inside and out."

"Oh, never mind." He released her arm, dabbing his brow again. "I just thought you might feel better about Sundays if we talked this over."

Her shell toughened further, if possible. "It's been many Sundays since Brent died. Why now? What's come over you?"

"It's not important. Not an exercise for us after all."

A knowing glint hardened her eyes. "I knew hanging around that coffee shop would corrupt your discipline."

"Oh, c'mon!"

"How I battled Brent to put you in a more exclusive high school. How thrilled I was to ship you off to Harvard after graduation to finally mingle exclusively with your own kind."

"Don't go blaming the Johnsons for what you see as my shortcomings."

"Do you deny that they're behind this soap-opera confessional brainstorm of yours today?"

"Shari and Dylan are open with each other. It may have rubbed off."

"Such displays are cheap."

"Not really. And you do have a problem with Sundays."

"All these years…you've seemed content enough."

"I have been, Mother. But I would like to settle down and have a family. I am thirty."

"That can be done with a modicum of restraint, some attention to your station." She cocked her head with a razor smile. "Surely Flame can offer you everything you need. Good breeding with an element of excitement. She played the role to perfection, stimulating and classy."

"Yes. And I told you days ago that the Beanery was my best bet for finding her."

"Tell me you've had some results."

"Afraid not." He had wisely decided not to tell Gwen of Flame's note. Like Dylan, Gwen would take the rejection to heart, would want to prepare some counterattack to draw Flame into the open. Between the two matchmakers, Garrett would be guaranteed no privacy in his romantic bumbling.

Her pencil form had sagged with his news. "Oh, Garrett! Sometimes I think you torment me on purpose."

"I gave it my best shot and failed."

"That's hard to believe. There must be a way to find her through that key ring—through that god-awful shop!"

"Maybe it will happen someday. I'm certainly not through with the Johnsons. I plan to be a regular there from here on in, renew my friendships with the old crowd. If Flame happens to show up during one of my visits, all the better. But I'm going to take on a new relaxed attitude about it, no more of those rigid appointments."

"So you're determined to slide back into that middle-class world. It's as though you're funneling the energy meant for Flame into that old connection."

Hating to see the Johnsons maligned, he revealed more than he planned. "But the connections are all tangled together. You and Dylan actually have the same goal where Flame is concerned. He'd love to see me hook up with her, would love to meet her himself. As we speak, he's struggling to come up with a plan B to replace the failed coffee dates."

"Is he really?" There was a new and genuine lilt to her voice.

"You might like both the Johnsons better now," he chided.

"What about the sister? She as giggly and useless as she used to be?"

"No, she's coming along nicely as an adult."

"Oh. Yes. She would be maturing."

Garrett could have allowed his lids to fall and summoned a splendid vision of Shari. But his observant mother would have spotted his mood shift and flown off the handle. As things stood, Gwen regarded Shari Johnson as a backstreet waif, a peppy adolescent who danced and jumped rope between the shop's tables and stroked Garrett's Brady High letterman jacket with childlike reverence.

"So, dear, are we on for the movies?"

"Sure, Mother."

"For the surface enjoyment of it, I mean to say, without any Freudian undercurrents."

He nodded solemnly. "No more maudlin attempts to care, I promise."

"Oh, how you twist things around!"

Garrett touched her rouged cheek, still wishing they could dig deeper. "You see what's playing while I clean up."

8

SHARI IMMEDIATELY RECOGNIZED Gwen McNamara breezing into the shop the following Wednesday afternoon. The matron rode in on a reminiscent ill wind, decidedly chilly beneath her designer clothes and fine jewelry. She dropped at least another ten degrees while pausing to take in the atmosphere, which really hadn't changed much since her last visit more than a decade ago.

Dylan would be on break off the premises, Shari silently lamented. Somehow getting the upper hand, yanking Gwen's pearls seemed a two-Johnson job.

It was silly to still feel intimidated by the woman, but the sensitive child in Shari couldn't help herself. And what if Gwen blew her cover? Took one look and recognized Shari as Flame? Gwen would no doubt explode and level the whole city block! Distraught as a thirteen-year-old once more, Shari slipped behind a coffee urn, reaching out to tap Tracy on the shoulder. "New customer!"

Tracy's round cheery face puckered. "You wish."

"What?"

Together they peeked at the matron lingering stiffly near the entrance, as though fortifying herself for battle. "I recognize Gwen McNamara from her picture in the society column just last week. She was at some groundbreaking ceremony wearing that same Anne Klein coat."

"You have a sharp eye," Shari muttered. "Too sharp."

"There aren't many coats like that in here. It's worth at least as much as your beaded red dress."

"Hey, that's not my red dress," Shari hissed. "It's Flame's. And we're not supposed to know about it, because it belonged to Garrett's secret date."

Tracy hit the heel of her hand on her temple, making her shiny black bangs bounce. "Right. Lost my head there for a minute."

"Wait on her," Shari beseeched.

"You know it's not that simple. She's not here for a salami sandwich or an espresso. She's here to kick some Johnson butt." Tracy pumped her skinny arm, as though showing off some bulk. "This is what you need to show her, girl."

"What if she makes the connection between me and you-know-who?"

"Garrett kissed you and he didn't figure it out."

Shari kept one eye on Gwen as she continued to whisper. "Women are better about detail, though. Furthermore, she told me on the yacht that she's a true theater buff. Odds are she might have a better-than-average idea of what I'd look like toned down."

"You'll have to chance it with her sooner or later."

"Later would be best."

"If her prejudice for you is as strong as you say, odds are good she'll flat out refuse to suspect."

"C'mon, be a good employee."

"Until you offer hazard pay, I'm better off playing the chicken." With that, Tracy flounced to the opposite end of the display case to serve a couple of young men in suits.

Gwen was advancing down the center aisle now, her lightweight tan coat billowing a bit to reveal a smart floral blouse and black linen skirt. Shari steeled herself behind the display case for the inevitable confrontation. To her surprise, though, the matron made a surprising maneuver, abruptly swinging into the cozy furniture area and the Club Wed station.

She'd come to check out the dating service, it seemed. She was probably mystified as to why Garrett had had such rotten luck in tracking down his fantasy lover.

Shari knew she should be finding great humor in the irony—that the McNamaras' beloved Flame existed right under their noses but their lofty self-images prevented them from seeing her.

But it was mainly with trepidation that Shari approached the Club Wed section. Should she pretend not to recognize Gwen after all these years? Even that small decision made her palms sweat.

Gwen solved the problem by calling her by name. If you counted "that Johnson girl" as a name. "I am Garrett's mother," she added on a note of pride. "Surely you remember."

Shari pretended to let it all click in her mind. "Oh, yes." She shook Gwen's hand, feeling the cut of her large ruby cluster ring, the withering appraisal in her gray eyes. Garrett's eyes were very similar to his mother's in size and color, yet hers were stonier somehow. Guess it was all in how one used them.

So far so good, Shari decided. Presumably Gwen had no idea that she was speaking condescendingly to the same fiery goddess she'd worshipped a mere two weeks ago. Shari was overcome with relief, reenergized by her power to manipulate. After all the times Gwen had made her feel insignificant when she was young, it was too tempting not to toy with her again, as she had on the yacht.

"I thought I'd stop in and see how this Club Wed operated."

Shari beamed proudly. "A very popular service with Manhattan's singles."

She was openly perplexed. "So I've come to understand. I did a little asking around, just to see what Garrett had gotten himself into." Gwen tapped her chin with a pearl-tipped talon, perusing the blue index cards. "I don't see Garrett's card up here. Can you explain?"

"Why, he's dropped out of the club," Shari explained with some surprise. "Didn't he mention it?"

"I know he stopped those daily coffee dates, but to remove himself from the club entirely seems...drastic."

Shari grinned, thinking how important Gwen made the club sound. A slam dunk for the home team. "He is a free man over twenty-one."

"Way over. That's the point. It's time he settled down." She clamped her thin red lips together, as though she'd said more than she intended.

Shari leaned closer in a conspiratorial manner, noting that Gwen didn't welcome the intimate gesture as she had with Flame. "From what he's told me, Garrett seems content enough with his life."

"Has my son been confiding in you?"

"Oh, yes, quite a lot."

Gwen surveyed her with a pitying *tsk.* "I suppose his search would capture the imagination of one closed in here day after day. You did hang on him quite a lot in the old days as I recall. Didn't he call you the split pea or something?"

Shari gritted her teeth. "Everyone around here has shown an interest. And I do have a life of my own, believe me."

"Of course you do." Gwen shifted from patronizing to businesslike with a smooth turn of gears. "Now then, about your club. The first order of affairs is to get Garrett's index card back on this board. Do you still have it?"

"Yes, we keep all the old cards, store them in our files along with member registration." She drew a hesitant breath. "But it seems to me that if Garrett doesn't want it posted—"

"What harm can it cause? A little unwanted mail coming his way is no big deal. Why not leave the option open for Flame if she wishes to write?"

Shari was surprised by Gwen's line of reasoning. It suggested that Garrett had kept Gwen in the dark about the brush-off note he received. Resenting Gwen's heavy-handedness herself, she was compelled to aid Garrett in his deception. "Certainly Flame would've bagged him by now if she had any intention of doing so. I think Garrett's right in wanting to soft-pedal the search. The attention it's brought seems to embarrass him."

"*You* think?" Gwen's voice was a dry-ice blast. "Why, Miss Johnson, you can't begin to understand the value of what we are searching for here. This mystery woman is a mother's dream-come-true for her son. She's clever, captivating, worldly. Too bad if Garrett is uneasy about using aggressive, stick-to-it methods. I will get the results for him. He will thank me on his wedding day."

Shari made an exaggerated O with her mouth. "She sure sounds awesome, larger than life."

Gwen missed the mockery in her tone. "Perhaps I've underestimated you. Perhaps you can be made to understand."

"I do have my clever moments."

"A relief to be sure. Now get cracking on that card."

Having had her jollies, Shari saw no choice but to meekly obey. Did anyone ever defy this steamroller?

Since the huge plastic file box was stored in a drawer under the cash register, Shari usually crouched right there to dig for the card. She began thumbing through the index only to find Gwen overhead, wedged between two stools, leaning over the pumpkin-colored counter. Her proximity was unnerving, causing Shari to pop to her feet empty-handed.

"Say, would you like a cup of coffee while you wait, Mrs. McNamara? My treat."

Gwen was slightly taken aback by the polite offer. "I suppose I could do with a cup. Plain black coffee, mind. Nothing gooey or frothy."

"Sure." She patted the counter. "Sit right here. The stools are rather comfortable."

"Yes," she drawled, sliding her tight rear end onto a round black vinyl seat. "I remember them from 1985."

Shari set a cup of steamy brew before her. "We are intending to completely remodel."

"Yes," Gwen said wearily, "your mother said the very same thing back in 1985. She never did change as much as her frumpy hairdo."

That was it. Nobody cut down her sweet mother. Shari was finished handling this dragon with kid gloves. "I'll be right back," she snapped. Bending over to lift the file box out of the open drawer, she disappeared into the back room.

Garrett's records were easy enough to find. Shari pulled out the blue index card meant for the board, and the complementing one holding personal information, including a work phone number. Scooping up the receiver, she punched in Garrett's private number.

"Hello, Garrett McNamara."

"Hello to you."

"Shari?" His tone held friendly surprise.

"That's right. And guess who's holding court out front in the shop?"

"Flame?" Friendly surprise instantly turned to a desperate and desirous gush. "Did she finally show up?"

"It's the other woman in your life," she corrected with fiendish pleasure.

"Mother," he guessed after a pause.

"The one and only. Gwen's right out on the floor as we speak, on the verge of having the place condemned."

"I am so sorry. But she's definitely not there to shut you down."

"Far from it! She's taking over the hunt for her fantasy daughter-in-law!"

He sighed heavily. "I thought I could fend her off by keeping Flame's note from her, but I guess I tripped up by talking you Johnsons up. She probably got it in her head that you were approachable."

"That almost seems like a compliment."

"It is."

"Well, approachable or not, she's been treating me like the village idiot, even called me split pea."

"She probably mistook your nickname—"

"Naturally! And don't you dare say it."

"I am so sorry about her."

"Fine. But can you come get her?"

"Please remain calm."

"Ha! She insulted my mother. Up until then, I was handling her, helping you. But she had no right—"

"Agreed. Now, can you tell me exactly what she's trying to do."

"Take over your love life. She looked over the club and has insisted I post your card on the board again."

"No way!"

"She's making me do it!"

"Nobody can make you do anything."

"How the hell do you know? If I were invincible, I

wouldn't be hiding out in the back of my own shop, whispering to you on the telephone."

"Have you tried the power of positive thinking?"

"I'm positive that I'm about to explode over all your shenanigans!"

"But why would you feel—"

His words were cut off as Shari slammed down the receiver.

She returned to the front of the shop to find Gwen polishing silverware she was never going to use with a paper napkin. "Excellent," she said at the sight of the blue index card in Shari's hand. "Now, go post it."

Shari was tempted to rip up the card in defiance. It would most likely drive Gwen off for now. But she was suddenly overwhelmed by the urge to punish the male McNamara instead. Garrett should have agreed to come once he knew all the facts. Sure, he was a busy man. But he would have come if Flame had been here.

Why, this whole shake-up in the shop was all his doing!

Fueled by high-octane sexual frustration, she marched to the dating station, held the card up and moved it across the board as Gwen called out instructions, trying to decide where her son would sit best.

"Hold it!" she finally ordered. "Push that tack in right there."

To their mutual surprise, a round of applause rose in the coffee shop. Apparently everyone was getting a kick out of the fussy stranger, as out of place seated at the chipped counter as the queen of England would be. Shari took it all in with fiendish humor, wending her way through the furniture with half curtsies.

"Look here!" Gwen clutched Shari's arm as she passed by the stools.

Shari's stomach tensed. "Just harmless fun, Mrs. Mc-Namara."

"No, girl, no. I mean—look at the door. The door!"

Shari glanced toward the entrance, seeing nothing unusual, no one but Magda gliding in dressed in a jade leotard covered by a light cotton wrap, her turquoise-tinted hair put up in a tight topknot. The image wasn't regular street wear, but striking and so very Magda. The actress had a great body for her age and had been in wearing less, especially on rehearsal days. "We don't have a formal dress code—"

"Is that or is that not Magda DuCharme?" Gwen demanded in an urgent hush.

"Well, sure. She's in here all the time." Only then did Shari catch the reverence in Gwen's manner, the soft sparkle in her stony eyes. "She's a good friend of mine, too," she couldn't resist adding smugly.

"May miracles never cease!" Gwen squeezed her arm harder. "You must introduce us."

Magda had paused to hail some fellow actors but answered Shari's summons immediately. Shari disengaged Gwen's jeweled claw from her arm as she made the introductions.

"I do like your son," Magda crooned bluntly. "He's macho terrific."

Perhaps for the first time ever, Gwen didn't immediately acknowledge a compliment to her prized child. "I may very well be your biggest fan, Ms. DuCharme."

Magda trained her vivid Gypsy eyes smugly on Shari. *So this is the pompous twit who gives you such trouble.* "Really?" Magda chortled. "I have so many."

"Of course you do," Gwen gushed, too starstruck to note Magda's mocking attitude. "And why not? All these years of stellar performances worldwide. *The Boyfriend* at Paris' Théâtre Antoine in 1965, *Hello Dolly* in Vi-

enna's Theater an der Wien in 1968. Not to mention all
the Broadway shows—*A Chorus Line, Cats, A Streetcar
Named Desire.* I've seen them all and countless others."

Magda bowed her head, her ego swelling. "I thank
you very much. You certainly know your theater trivia."

"What are you doing now, Ms—"

"Do call me Magda, Gwen." Magda sank onto the
stool beside her, causing Gwen to gasp in joy. "I am involved in a small show called *Bottoms Down.* It's very
naughty and daring and fun."

"When does it open?"

"In a month." Magda glowed in ecstasy. "I can't
wait."

"Nor can I!"

Shari rounded the counter to wait on a customer, wondering what rich folk called a squeal like the one that just
erupted from Gwen. She wrapped up two ham sandwiches and bagged them with two mineral waters, made
the appropriate change, then quickly went about getting
Magda her favorite cappuccino. Shari set it on the
counter along with her elbows. "I was just telling
Mrs.—"

"Call her Gwen," Magda insisted cozily. "She won't
mind."

Gwen cleared her throat, her smooth forehead strain-
ing. "No, that's perfectly fine."

"Okay." Shari beamed, every bit as assured as Flame
at that moment in time. "Anyway, Gwen and I were just
discussing Garrett's search for his provocative mystery
woman."

"Even you know the story, Magda?" Gwen asked,
daring to hope.

Magda slid her saucer closer. "Certainly. This is my
roosting place, Gwen. A cherished second home."

"Really…" Gwen looked around the homey shop with a newly admiring eye.

"Quaint, yes?"

Gwen agreed with minor strain. "There is a certain savoir faire if one looks hard, in the right light."

Shari knew it shouldn't matter that Mrs. McNamara was begrudgingly giving the shop some due respect, but they deserved it. "Anyway, Mags," she persisted, "I was trying to prepare Gwen for a letdown. After all these days, it seems unlikely that Flame will reveal herself."

Magda lifted the huge cup to her mouth. "She certainly is a playful minx, hiding out."

"But is she hiding in the true sense of the word?" Gwen argued. "I've come to test a variation of that theory. I think she may be hiding right here under your very noses." Gwen gasped as Magda sloshed hot coffee on her wrist, quickly picking up her napkin to dab the other woman's skin. "You must be careful, Magda."

"Yes, Gwen." Magda avoided Shari's gaze, swabbing her pooling saucer with her own napkin. "How clumsy."

"How right." Shari frowned, forcing eye contact.

"And what a bonus to have your practiced eye to help test my theory, Magda. No one would understand Flame's game better than you, a true professional," Gwen asserted. "After all, she made herself up in grand actress style for the auction, completely transformed herself for a show."

Magda made a production of pondering. "I see."

"Then presumably she stripped off the layers and slipped back into her own gentler, but still lovely, persona."

"How poetically put." Magda pondered further. "If I am to fully understand, you're suggesting that Flame walks among us, and the untrained eyes have yet to spot her."

"Exactly!" Gwen rejoiced, actually snaking a bony arm around the actress. "I've come to size up this situation, hoping against hope," she said demurely, "to perhaps run into her myself."

"One visit would hardly do it," Magda blurted out.

Shari's eyes bored holes into her friend's, scolding her for another blunder. Shari certainly didn't want Gwen hanging around here, and encouraging as much was a mistake!

"One hundred more visits wouldn't necessarily make any difference," Shari objected coolly.

Gwen lifted her chin regally. "Few enough people have met Flame. I not only had the good fortune to spend some one-on-one time with her, but I have the rare experience and wisdom to imagine her in her natural state. In short, I may be Garrett's only chance. And if it means parking here to make our dreams come true—I shall."

Dylan had entered through the back and was standing behind Shari now. "Why, hello there, Mrs. M."

Magda worked her plum lips like a cat full of cream. "Wants you to call her Gwen."

Surprisingly, Gwen regarded Dylan with true joy. "Thank you for trying to help Garrett track down his new lady, Dylan. Your assistance has been invaluable, what with the communication your club offers." The faint lines fanning her eyes crinkled a trifle then in confusion. "Though it is a strange loop that brings my son's fortunes back here, of all places."

With a rush of empathy, Shari watched Dylan as Gwen scanned their humble establishment with a lingering trace of bewilderment. It shouldn't matter to Dylan what this woman thought; but like Shari, her brother couldn't shake the insecurities of the past when confronted with this powerful mother figure. The scars of childhood faded only so much, it seemed.

"We're remodeling the place," Dylan announced, his eyes darting over the wall-to-wall imperfections.

"So Garrett tells me."

"Commissioning Elite House for the project."

Gwen was visibly impressed. "A fine choice. They won't disappoint. Though," she added on a doubtful note, "their services can be expensive."

Dylan's arm swept lavishly. "We can afford it these days. Workin' well, workin' well."

Gwen smiled slyly. "It's certainly the key to hanging on to your higher class of patron."

Shari ran a sponge over the counter with jerky strokes, annoyed to see Dylan taking the backhanded compliment with grace. If only Gwen knew with whom she was dealing here. Shari stopped fretting long enough to savor the lighter side of this situation. Gwen's self-importance, her inability to identify Shari as the one she sought were nothing short of delicious.

Still, the result was more bittersweet than she liked. Shari tossed the sponge in the stainless steel sink with a sigh. The scenario didn't bring her the rush she hoped for. It was as sad as it was amusing. All her life she wanted to be Garrett's true love. Now that she'd loved and lost him, the dream was dying before her eyes, slowly, torturously, as the McNamaras refused to give up the ghost.

She wasn't sure how much more of this pretense she could take.

"There has to be a way to pump new life into our search," Dylan was telling the women as she focused on their conversation again. "I've been racking my brain with possibilities."

"I'm going on break now," Shari announced abruptly, having had her fill.

Dylan leaned over to ruffle her hair. "Aw, no, sis. I'm too tied up here to let you go."

"You went on break—left the premises."

He made an exasperated sound. "Look, I'll skip dinner completely and you can take extra time then." He made a shooing motion with his hand. "Just help serve now, okay?"

Shari smiled falsely, curling her fist. "Just don't be long." *And whatever you do, don't come up with any brilliant plan B.*

GARRETT ARRIVED at the coffee shop an hour later to a most unlikely sight: Dylan leaning over the inside of the counter, deep in conversation with two women seated on stools opposite—the actress Magda and his own conniving mother.

Spotting him, Shari wended her way through the tangle of tables. He absently noted that she was looking mighty cute in some slimmer-fitting jeans that did justice to her hips.

It seemed impossible that she and Flame would be pushing the same panic button inside him, considering their vast differences in personality and appearance. Still, there it was. He was attracted to both of them, intrigued by any secrets they might have.

But the idea of taking Shari to bed did cause him some hesitation. She'd always seemed so young when they were teens. Of course, maturity had bridged that gap—a mere four years wasn't much at the twenty-something level.

Half-ashamed, he thought how exciting it had been to have the showy Flame on his arm at his party, how easily she turned heads, how all the men had lusted for her.

Her being easy on the eyes had been easy on his ego, made their encounter so singeing, so fantastic. He'd never been so pumped during sex. Liquid fire had swelled him, driven him to dizzier heights of sensation. He shivered slightly under his gray linen suit as he longed to go there all over again.

But it was Shari who should be his main focus now. He noted that heads weren't turning upon her approach, but a regular girl like her couldn't be expected to cause a riot—few women would.

Garrett had sorted out the realities carefully. The man who committed to Shari would have to be content in adoring her on his own, being in a crowded room with knowledge that he alone was the only one imagining her with her clothes off. Not a half-bad position really, to possess a vibrant female body and soul, to see things in her that few other men would or could recognize at first glance. It suggested a deeper insight and higher intelligence.

To be absolutely fair to the absent Flame, though, she might also possess many of the same qualities beneath the bonus glitter.

At this place in time, Garrett was certain he couldn't go wrong with either woman.

"Oh, Garrett, you came!"

Garrett found Shari's ability to readjust her feelings a rare godsend. She'd been so angry on the phone, but his compliance brought her back around. "I got to thinking you were right to insist."

Garrett flinched a little as Shari touched his suit-jacket sleeve. Her smallest gestures sent electricity through his system, as did her sassy talk. He'd been tied in knots since her phone call. All the way over in the taxi, he was trying to read between the lines, figure out if she took him seriously.

Did he even have a right to wonder, though, what with all this fuss being made over Flame?

"So, Mom turn every screw in the place yet?" he half teased.

Glancing over at the counter where the threesome huddled, Shari grew dazed. "Believe it or not, she's found an ally. In Dylan."

Garrett was baffled. "I understand what Gwen wants with Dylan, since he's furthering her matchmaking cause. But why would Dylan give her the time of day? He's been having a great time with this mystery all on his own. He doesn't need her help."

She flashed him a wistful smile. "He thinks he needs something far more important from Gwen, her approval."

"Why?"

"She was the only mother from the old crowd who didn't approve of him."

Garrett scratched his chin. "That kind of vulnerability sounds dangerous."

"That ain't all that's dangerous." She paused to watch him squirm. "He's told her about the note you got."

"Dammit."

"Told you to come right away."

"I bet I would've had to fly to stop that revelation from pouring out of your blabbermouth brother."

"Well, had you hurried, you might have at least put a stop to plan B."

He paled. "They've got one already?"

"The last time I passed by they were considering advertisement strategies, billboard coverage, newspaper ads, lots of ways to serve you up as fresh bait."

"As if Flame can be reeled in." Garrett stalked over to the counter, standing behind his mother's stool.

She swiveled around with a cry of elation. "How nice, dear!"

"Is it?" he asked dryly. "What brings you to this part of town?"

Gwen was determinedly blissful. "You won't believe my fortune, running into the stunning Magda Du-Charme here of all places! She is a legend in the theater—a true actress from the old school."

Garrett smiled thinly at the capricious Magda. "How are you today?"

"Splendid," Magda rasped dramatically, running a suggestive eye over his form.

Something about Magda's response struck Garrett. Flame had spoken in the same lush way, stripped him naked in much the same manner. Was Flame's whole persona nothing more than a performance? Had anything about the woman been true and natural?

"I should be terribly angry with you," Gwen murmured to her son, smoothing his lapel. "Hiding Flame's note from me."

He spoke close to her ear with a deceptively pleasant tone. "I believe it's what they used to call a Dear John letter during the war. Nothing encouraging about it."

"It may all be part of the game."

"All in all, it was a fairly convincing read."

Gwen was unswayed. "I took that key you found to a locksmith and he confirms that it is most likely for an outside door to a domicile."

"So what?"

"It stands to reason that the key-ring is important to her, that this place is important to her. As inventive as she is, she would at the very least want to spy on you, gauge the progress you're making with her clue."

Garrett stiffened, embarrassed over the very idea of being observed for some woman's amusement.

"Mother, I feel very strongly that speculation has gotten way out of hand."

"To the contrary, I'd say we have it well in hand," Gwen crowed, indicating her male accomplice across the counter.

Taking an obvious cue, Dylan cleared his throat. "I'm pleased to announce that Gwen and I have come up with a plan B. Something that will boost Club Wed's profile and will no doubt smoke out the lovely Flame."

"What's that?" Shari and Garrett chorused.

"A party. A matchmaking get-together. All the members of Club Wed will be invited to a blowout. They'll all wear tags bearing their first names and four digit club codes. Members can mingle in person, match up index cards to faces without setting up a date. All Garrett has to do is step in and pluck Flame out from the bunch." Dylan rubbed his hands together. "Brilliant, eh?"

"What if she doesn't show?" Garrett demanded.

"We'll make the challenge too good to pass up," Dylan replied. "We're calling the dance, Blame the Flame. Only she will get the personal message, fully understand the game. Other members will think we're talking about general flames of passion. See?"

"And I will be there to help you find her, Garrett," Gwen offered placatingly. "No matter what her persona this round, she won't get away."

Shari couldn't believe the trouble they were going to. "Dylan, we haven't the money for such a party. Hotel ballrooms cost a fortune—"

"Whoa. Gwen has already come up with a solution."

Gwen tipped her head cockily to her son. "What do you say to having it at the Spotlight Academy?"

"Where we took those ballroom dance lessons?"

"Lily Fleur is an old friend. I'm sure she'll cooperate for a minimal fee, which I'll gladly pay myself."

The plan slipped too easily from his mother's mouth. "You already called her, didn't you?" Garrett asked flatly.

"Yes, as a matter of fact I did." Gwen grasped her son's hand. "Why don't you go over there and check the place out. It means so much to Lily that you pay a visit yourself. Apparently you were one of her best pupils."

"I'll come with you," Dylan offered, "representing the shop and all."

"No." Garrett ground the word out. "I feel railroaded enough as it is." He paused to listen to his gut, a practice that served him well professionally. "I'd like Shari to come with me."

Shari gulped, pressing a hand to her chest. "Me?"

"Sure, you danced there, too, remember?"

It was his memory she was worried about, especially the short term. Shari suddenly felt as if she were sinking in quicksand. Bits of the puzzle kept falling onto the table: the found apartment key and her loss of a key, the way she and her alter ego kissed. Put her back on the dance floor with Garrett, bodies locked together, moving in perfect sync, and who knew what would jog loose in his brain!

"Of course she'll go along," Dylan assured, eager to please his pal. "Tell Lily a Saturday in late May would be nice. See what kind of terms you can come to." He clapped a hand on Garrett's sturdy shoulder. "Get moving, guys. Time's a-wastin'."

9

THE MISSION to Spotlight Academy didn't get started as swiftly as the ever vocal Dylan would have liked. Shari took pleasure in slowing her brother down by stuffing a cranberry bagel into his mouth. She then declared that she wanted to change clothes and scooted up to her apartment before he could chomp himself free.

Magda, eager to escape, as well, begged off the clingy Gwen McNamara and followed Shari up the old wooden staircase to the second floor.

Pausing at her door, Shari dug into her blue-jean pocket for her new Beanery key ring and slid it into the lock. With a twist and turn, they were in. They didn't speak until the door was closed firmly behind them. Shari tried to look exasperated but couldn't help chiming in with her self-appointed fairy godmother's husky laughter.

"So that's the old dragon who tortured you as a child!"

"That's a bit of an exaggeration," Shari protested.

"Not by much, I imagine." The thespian's wrap flowed around her slender leotard-clad body as she struck a stubborn pose. "This old pro can easily chart her motivation—from her twenty-four-carat cradle."

"Well, she sure was pleased to discover you frequent the shop," Shari marveled, moving through the small living room toward her bedroom.

Magda was right on her heels with a flourish. "She

does know her theater. Not that that forgives everything."

Shari opened the accordion door to her closet, glancing back with a wry grin. "You were in heaven down there, basking in her admiration like a cat stretched out in sunshine."

Magda's lined face glowed under its makeup. "True. Admiration is my fuel. But you should be enjoying her as much as I am. To see the mighty McNamara machine grovel for me and for Flame. Such a bonus to our one-trick pony of a night."

"It is satisfying on a lot of levels," Shari agreed, thumbing through her hangers. What to wear to that old dance studio? "But Gwen still has a way of diminishing me, Shari Johnson. And I'm not so bad, even without the fantasy shell."

Magda nodded, fully understanding. "Rather sad, of course, that her nose is too high in the air to see the genuine beauty only inches away at eye level." She placed a hand on her bony hip. "Though her gushing over your alter ego makes a lasting mockery of every prejudice she has."

"I know." Shari sighed wistfully. "That part is very satisfying."

"So what is the matter?"

"Garrett, of course!"

"You are impossible to please, darling. Even now you are preparing to go out with him."

"But the idea that a relationship between us could ever work out is too far-out. Knowing that plain truth makes time with him painful." She shook her head, pressing fingers to temples.

Magda, acting as any godmother worth her salt would, was nothing short of infuriated. "Ha! You profess yourself a dreamer when you barely take a chance."

"I take chances! Took one big one, anyway," she conceded under Magda's demanding look.

"So your one-night stand has turned into something more. Go with it in the hope that the ultimate dream could work out, that a happily-ever-after is possible." Magda sidestepped the bed, reaching out to pinch Shari's chin. "Wouldn't you rather make a run for him than sit around the rest of your life, clutching your secret conquest to your chest, reliving that one passionate encounter over and over and over again?"

"I never dared to consider—"

Magda pinched her chin harder then released it, sending Shari toppling to the mattress. "So dare now! It isn't too late. It's right on time, in fact. Garrett's ripe for the picking, full of confusion as he pines for Flame and wrestles with a new attraction to you. The poor dolt's most vulnerable as he struggles to figure through the whys."

"But he's gaining ground," Shari asserted, "examining his attraction to two women at once. I think he's just a breath away from merging our images." As long as she was seated on the bed, she removed her sensible work shoes and anklets. "And what were you thinking, encouraging this plan to lure Flame out of hiding? Can't you see how much tougher it will make it for plain old Shari?"

Magda was rarely contrite, but this was one of those moments in which she had the grace to mumble a half apology. "I was caught up in the fairy-tale romance of the moment."

Indignant, Shari popped up again. "I've given up the Cinderella kick and want you to, as well. It really doesn't fit this situation, after all."

Magda's mouth curved slyly as she plucked a pretty yellow sundress off the clothing rack. "But the lost key to this apartment serves so well as your glass slipper."

"Ah, but that particular prince wasn't toyed with unmercifully after the ball. I took off a lot more than my high heels that night on the yacht. I seduced Garrett with teasing and lies."

Magda pressed the dress to Shari's body, favoring the result. "So this is the ultramodern version of the tale."

Shari yanked the dress away, taking it off the hanger. "Don't miss my point, Magda. The original prince was not set up the way Garrett was. Garrett is bound to feel like a total fool when he discovers that I've been playing him from two different angles."

"Surely even this twist can be set to your advantage," Magda insisted, bending over to pluck some white sandals from the shoe rack on the closet floor. "Try to exploit the thrill of holding tight to your secret, the constant threat of discovery. Might make for the hottest tryst imaginable. You'll easily outsizzle Flame."

Shari pulled her knit work shirt over her head and deftly tossed it into a laundry basket set beside the old maple dresser. "You are notorious."

"It's only a temporary game in any case. The feelings growing between you and Garrett are bound to strengthen with time," Magda said in a gentler tone. "He'll forget all about Flame, concentrate solely on you."

Shari stripped off her jeans and sent them to the basket. "Even so, you know full well that Gwen would never accept me under any circumstances."

"Forget her role for now. I will handle her for you. Go for Garrett all out, dance the mating dance for real, with a future in mind—as Shari!"

"I would love to do that. But the mating glitch is where the most trouble lies," Shari sought to explain. "Kissing him was risky enough, but to indulge in sex…he'd surely recognize me then."

Magda froze, ultimately stumped. "I hadn't thought in those terms. Maybe some tint, some bikini wax, some tanning lotion—"

"No! It wouldn't be enough. People make love in different ways. He'd be certain to make the connection." Ruefully, Shari tugged the dress over her head.

Magda tugged up her back zipper. "Can't you behave differently, change your method of operation?"

"You already know I pulled out all the stops," Shari stated bluntly. "I can't regress, give him half myself. He'd sense I was holding back and think he was doing something wrong."

"Of course. And people have their own unique taste and texture, which would be impossible to fake. How shortsighted of me not to see the whole picture right away." Magda was thoughtful, sympathetic. "Perhaps if you waited, say, six months. His memories would be faded enough to give you a fresh beginning."

Shari smiled falsely. "That might have done it. Garrett seemed tired of the search, well on the way to giving up. But then we butted in to stir things up—first me with my goodbye note and now you helping to arrange a trap for Flame, forcing her back into the limelight."

"I mostly just approved of their plans."

"Still, you were in cahoots. And what an effective trap it is."

Magda waved her hand. "Not necessarily. So Flame doesn't show up at this Club Wed party."

"That's no good. Now that Dylan and Gwen have banded together, there will be no end to the matchmaking attempts. If I don't show up, they'll go on to orchestrate a plan C, then D, then E. Somehow I have to put a stop to this hunt this time, bring closure to Flame."

Magda reached for the beaded red dress hanging on

the end of the rod in a plastic garment bag. "So I guess this will be put into service one more time, eh?"

Shari glared at the dress she once adored. "Thanks to you, yes."

THE SPOTLIGHT ACADEMY of Ballroom Dance proved to be virtually unchanged with the passage of a dozen years. On Fifty-third Street above a shoe store, it was still a bright and open place of bleached woods, tall windows and high ceilings.

Lily Fleur was as gracious as ever as she slid open the steel door to greet them. Dressed for a lesson in one of her trademark chiffon numbers, lilac with a full skirt and ruffled collar, she could have just as well fox-trotted right out of the 1980s.

Or so Garrett told her. Shari quickly noted an extra ten pounds around Lily's middle and the silver streaks in her auburn curls, putting her at the cusp of the millennium looking every bit of forty-five.

Garrett was being extra kind, was all, and Shari was impressed that he'd think to bother.

"And you two!" Lily's plump cheeks bunched as she surveyed them. "So adult, so graceful. Why, you just oozed into the room side by side. Natural partners still."

Color splashed Garrett's jaw, but he didn't look displeased. "I don't know how much my mother told you…"

Lily's pale blue eyes glittered in a more businesslike way. "That you want to rent my place for some sort of mixer. By all means, we can arrange something. I'm always closed on Saturday nights anyway."

Garrett expelled a breath of relief. Then Lily didn't know about Flame. That would cut back on all the awkward questions. As it stood, he was half-tempted to cut back on the whole awkward dance fiasco itself, focus exclusively on this modest, unambiguous, reliable lady at his side.

Forget the daring, sexy, unreliable Flame for good.

The idea brought him a sense of relief. But would such relief last? Could he give her up so easily without one last look to be sure? Even now, forbidden images sprang to life: Garrett lying on his belly, Flame's strong fingers massaging his back, sliding lower to his buttocks, squeezing his hard muscles, sliding between his thighs, ever so slowly discovering his sex, bringing him to erection. Her fingernails had been false, but she sure knew how to use them....

His eyes slanted to Shari, standing beside him with a serene look. She had so many qualities a man could appreciate, tolerance, compassion, a quick wit and boundless energy. She would make a man a fine wife. But there'd be few surprises, he wagered.

What had happened to the playful, capricious side he remembered? Now she was an open book for all to read, practically right down to her estimate for Elite House. Did she ever splurge on anything fanciful? Yearn for something outrageous? Garrett was considered rather stuffy at times with his workaholic attitude, but Shari's conservatism made him look like a daredevil.

Lily waltzed across the room, summoning them to her partitioned work space. Shari had to admit the instructor was still light on her dyed-to-match pumps, despite the puffy tire at her waistline. Lily sat down at her old wooden desk and pulled open her appointment book. She half turned in her creaky chair to smile up at the pair. "Too bad you weren't here an hour ago. I was instructing David Crain's daughters. You remember David from the kiddie cotillions I held here on Sunday afternoons."

Shari had instant recollection. "Ah, yes, I'm afraid I had to sink my heel into David's instep as he patted me down during a tango. Apparently he just had to know if I was wearing a bra. Bet he feels differently about inquiring young male minds now that he has little dancers of his own."

Garrett's laughter mingled with Lily's, but he was wistful, too. That burst of spunk was a fine example of the young Shari he'd liked so well back then. He saw hints of her now, like when they discussed his bumbling attempt to find Flame through those coffee-break appointments at the shop. How she'd disapproved while pretending not to care! But for the most part, it was as though she were on permanent restraint. Afraid of releasing something, revealing something...

The last Saturday in May was decided upon for the dance. Garrett brought his checkbook out of an inside pocket in his gray jacket and paid the rent in full with a flourish of pen. He expected Shari to put up a fuss, but she didn't. Her body squirmed a little under her lemony, form-fitting dress, but she made not a peep of protest. Recalling her concerns over the cost of the decorator, he was beginning to wonder if she was having serious cash-flow problems. But that was highly unlikely. The Johnsons, with the hand-me-down shop and aunt's inheritance, had never been better heeled.

Lily's next lesson arrived minutes later as they played catch-up, a man about Lily's age with a bald spot, polyester-blend slacks and shirt and what appeared to be two left feet. "One of Manhattan's finest, kiddies," Lily murmured as she breezed by. "Protecting us while we sleep."

A tough cop off the night shift taking dipping orders from sweet Lily? Garrett and Shari shared a conspiratorial smirk.

Lily wasted no time. With a briskly cheery greeting to Detective Winters, she swished over to the entertainment center and turned on the music. There was a familiar pause in the recording, giving pupil and student time to get into the dance position.

"Join us for the cha-cha!" Lily urged, clamping a hand on Winters's shoulder.

Shari froze in smile and spine. Back on the yacht they'd danced to another of Lily's favorites, "The Peanut Vendor." Would Garrett pick up on her similar moves in this different setting? She would have little choice but to find out. Garrett had wasted no time whisking her into his arms as a rendition of "Cherry Pink and Apple Blossom White" pumped out loud and clear from the ceiling speakers.

Shoes clattered on the hardwood flooring. The detective was rather clumsy, putting a cramp in Lily's flawless style. But Shari and Garrett moved in perfect, if slightly uneasy, harmony.

Garrett immediately sensed the hesitancy in Shari's body language during that first dance. But what a body. This was the first time he'd gotten a decent glimpse of the shape she'd kept so well hidden. It felt good to plant a firm hand on her slender waist. Felt flamin' good.

To Shari's credit, she was every bit as shapely as Flame, every bit as graceful. But to Flame's credit, she didn't have Shari's dance history with him to fall back on; still, she'd fallen into his steps like magic.

Though, at this moment, with this woman, Garrett could hardly deny he felt bewitched, even besotted. He was determined they enjoy every minute of it and advised Shari to relax a bit more.

"Guess I'm nervous because it's been so long."

"I understand. But you never lose it."

Ironically, it was his acceptance of her lie that helped her relax. He was in no way prepared to make the obvious connection between his women.

A flight straight to heaven. It was the only description Shari had for this second chance to be in Garrett's arms. Ballroom dancing was a very athletic feat and, when done with a lover, a form of sex with clothes on. Shari was determined to get as much feeling out of the physical contact as possible. She followed his movements in rote fashion, reveling in the masterful way he guided her body. His lean, hard limbs offered near-irresistible enticement as they glided around the floor as one.

The more they exerted themselves, the stronger the chemistry between them. Shari sighed appreciatively, longing for his hands to caress her.

Garrett could have sworn he felt Shari's body shudder. Was she coming on to him? Seemed unlikely she'd take the chance with his infatuation for Flame a bigger issue than ever. Still, part of him wanted her to incinerate Flame in his mind, even though common sense told him that was a mighty selfish wish.

"I CAN'T BELIEVE WE STAYED the entire lesson!" Shari made the remark as they climbed into a cab in front of the Ed Sullivan Theater an hour later.

"It was fun," he said sincerely, cozying up next to her in the back seat.

"You wore me out."

"Maybe you'd like to take a raincheck on the tour of my apartment."

"No way, I'm still up for that." Shari settled back as the taxi pulled out from the curb. "I'd rather be away from the shop and my brother right now. The place is in a panic today, with Dylan ranting on about the remodeling, making a goof of himself trying to please your mother."

Garrett's brows jumped. "I still can't believe he's so set

on winning her over. Generally speaking, he acts more like a macho caveman than a needy kid."

Her voice took a clipped edge. "Emotions can be tricky. Like I told you before, it's always bothered him that Gwen thought so little of us."

"Mother speaks better of him now."

"Maybe, but she is using Dylan exclusively to track Flame, and it bothers me that he doesn't seem to fully realize that."

Garrett shifted uncomfortably on the car seat, unintentionally grazing her exposed thigh with his knee. The crisp linen on her skin sent a jolt through her system, which took effort to conceal. If only he'd admit that she affected him, that he found her exciting.

"Shari, I could deny—"

"Deny what!" She sat forward, suddenly eager, open, susceptible.

Garrett was stunned. What did she expect to hear? "You know," he stammered uncomfortably, "that Gwen's tough-hearted."

Shari sank a little into the opposite door. "Oh. Yes." Apparently he wasn't about to admit that kneeing her was a mind-blowing charge. Of course it would be nothing in comparison to sex with Flame. The fact that her alter ego had been just too darn potent under the sheets was certainly coming back to haunt her.

"Gwen is without a doubt a real pain about social amenities, the class structure, appearances…"

"Surface nothings," Shari offered in summation, tugging her dress over her legs.

"Well…yeah. But those things must mean something to Dylan, though, since he's trying so hard to spruce up your shop."

"That's called progress," Shari retorted, folding her arms across her chest. "Dylan wants to succeed, live comfortably, it's true. But believe me, he doesn't care how much your mother is worth, or exactly who at your country club she dines with. He mainly sees her as the only mother of the Brady High basketball team who didn't fall for his line way back when, who didn't fuss over him, approve of him."

"Unreal."

"You McNamaras are too hung up on money, Garrett, suspecting that everyone wants a part of you strictly because of it. Some of us have lived without the big bucks all along and still enjoy life. Okay?"

Chastened and rebuked, Garrett nodded tightly. He wasn't the world's most sensitive male, but it seemed like the wrong time to ask her if she'd somehow mismanaged her inheritance from Aunt Lucille. Her jumpiness on the subject of the Elite House and the expense of this singles party hinted that there was a cash-flow problem. He'd have to bide his time to broach the subject, preferably when she wasn't fuming over him being a paranoid moneymonger.

Peters had the door open to Garrett's penthouse even before he could fish his key chain out of his pocket.

"The doorman called ahead to say you were coming up with a lady," he intoned, a smile of approval centered upon Shari. "I just wasn't sure what to expect."

Garrett kept his sense of humor as he ushered Shari into the living room. "Gwen is what you expected, Peters. We can speak freely around Miss Johnson. She will fully understand any complaints."

Peters lifted the white sleeve of his jacket and checked his watch. "Mrs. McNamara's called numerous times, expecting your return. So has a male. The caller I.D. identified all the calls coming from some bean place. Does your mother have a new friend?"

Garrett winked at Shari. "In fact she does. And I must say they make mighty strange bedfellows."

"An unholy alliance," Shari bantered.

"Oil and water."

"May and December."

"Rags to riches."

They broke out in hearty laughter, their earlier tension over the mother-brother pair completely disintegrating.

Peters regarded them in surprise. "Am I missing something?"

"Not really." Garrett composed himself, loosening his tie. "As you know, Gwen's tracking my date from the auction with the determination of a seasoned bounty hunter."

Shari watched him tug the strip of black silk out from under his crisp white collar with a mild shiver of longing. The last time he'd removed a tie that way he was intent on making love to her. It was nonsense here and now, of course. Still, her body anticipated, yearned for it. She watched his fingers push shirt buttons through holes, remembering all the intimate places he'd invaded on her person. Garrett knew how to please a lover and took his sweet time doing it.

"You all right?"

His husky voice, tinged with concern, was startling. "Sure," she squeaked. *As all right as someone wearing panties three sizes too small for her.*

"I think I'll just go into the bedroom and change into more comfortable clothes."

She averted her gaze from his, envisioning exactly what he looked like in nude splendor. "I'll…wait."

"Great. If you want anything, tell Peters."

"A drink, perhaps, miss?" Peters asked genially.

"Something cool—cold." Shari shifted her macramé

shoulder bag from one arm to another. "Something very cold."

"An alcoholic beverage?"

"Very alcoholic," she confirmed sagely.

Garrett, meanwhile, was stripping off his suit jacket in the master suite. Shari was definitely harboring a sexual awareness for him, after all. There was no mistaking her carnal thoughts this time, the sheen in her eyes, the quiver of her mouth. She was letting go of her inhibitions, indulging in secret longings concerning the two of them. Even more surprising was how much her progress excited him.

Imagine, the String Bean, picturing him naked. What was the world coming to?

He sat on the bed and shucked off his dress shoes and socks. Her expression was best described as a tentative ogle. But ogles weren't meant to be half-baked, almost regretted. They were supposed to be bold, singeing, certain.

So how was he supposed to take this timid come-on? Pretend he didn't notice?

Try and tell that to his body. Standing up, he shucked off his trousers. The strain to his briefs was clearly visible. He began to tug at the cuffs of his shirt, working the quandary through. Okay, so mild-mannered Shari was interested, but hesitant. A little sassy when she let go, but keeping her emotions under some crazy kind of house arrest.

Garrett prided himself on understanding the women he dated, of figuring out their needs and doing his best to satisfy. But never in recent memory could he recall a woman so complicated.

Fortunately, they did share one comfort zone already. Out on the dance floor. The partnership of old came flooding back; the meld of their bodies, the timing, the unison. They'd always had an instinctive feel for each other in dance, the recent barriers had all simply fallen away like a slippery cloak.

Same with Flame.

The reminder wasn't a welcome one right now, with Shari waiting for him in the next room. After acknowledging Shari's charming, lustful awakening, he felt kind of cheap going back once again to compare her to the more experienced woman. She deserved to be judged on her own merits, which were numerous.

Maybe, just maybe, Shari could be taught the art of seduction, of reckless love play. If only he could encourage her to release the explosive energy she stubbornly suppressed. There had to be a button to push. A key to unlock. A man would have a good time making that discovery. A very good time indeed.

10

GARRETT RETURNED to the living room to find Shari sipping on the last of a martini and studying a collage on the cream-colored wall. Peters had discreetly disappeared to see to the laundry.

"Newly discovered artist in the Village," he explained, sidling close. Shari always smelled so fresh, so sweet. Like springtime itself.

Shari couldn't help noting how wonderful he looked in a white terry V-neck pullover and lightweight slacks, in that appealing zone between formality and grunge. And he was openly admiring her yellow sundress all over again. "I've never seen metal chips lacquered to a canvas before," she said conversationally, struggling to keep her cool. It was hard to concentrate on the mundane when they were only steps away from his bedroom. She imagined he had a king-size bed, comparable to the one on the yacht.

He gestured to the gritty spray set against the sky-blue oil background. "It's a representation of the brutal hailstorm of life. The struggle of man against nature."

"No kidding." She squinted harder. "I think this guy needs a caffeine jolt from my shop, some fresh focus."

Garrett was amused. "I'll tell him." He took Shari's empty glass and moved behind the portable bar in the corner of the room. A feeling of warmth infused him as he realized that Shari had followed.

He half turned to find her directly behind him, in fact.

He couldn't help teasing her a bit. "Still the tagalong, I see."

"I'm a natural behind the scenes, I suppose."

Peters had left a shaker of martinis on the ready, so it was easy to set up twin drinks on the teak bar. Garrett took his time playing bartender, measuring his words. Seemed she'd given him a decent opening for a heart-to-heart chat.

"I'm kind of surprised to hear you admit to that in such an offhand way."

"The behind-the-scenes stuff?" Her pale brows arched. "Why?"

"Well, that night in your apartment, when you were bickering with Dylan, you talked of wanting to explore options outside the shop. I was fascinated."

He was actually bothering to listen to the things she said to other people, even musing over them! "I'd like to branch out eventually," she admitted. "I don't know when that will be, though. Dylan relies on me, you see. He roars like a lion, but it's all an act. He's a big tender cat underneath, who needs my emotional support."

"All the more reason why he should use his own dating service to find a mate to torture."

Shari laughed. "Yeah, I agree. But for now, he's too busy playing Cupid for everybody else."

Garrett sipped his drink, feeling hesitant. Funny, it was so unlike him to feel the least bit awkward in this sort of intimate situation. He was generally glib and sure of himself. Perhaps it was lingering knowledge that Shari knew his weaknesses. It wouldn't stop him from pressing on, though. "Dylan aside," he continued, "you must think of having a life of your own."

"I do have one!"

"But if it isn't just right—"

"Hey, I'm not the bore I seem." She clamped her mouth shut, realizing that had come out all wrong.

His gray eyes twinkled. "Trust me, Shari, you are not boring."

She ran a finger around the rim of her glass. "What I mean to say is, I'm doing fine."

"You seem frustrated," he persisted gently. "Uptight because things aren't going your way. Not fine at all."

How astute. How clever. How frustrating and flattering all at once. In one fell swoop he made her feel a unique treasure and a naive dupe in need of a guardian. "I will see to my dreams," she asserted. "Someday."

They were no longer kids, though. Someday was today. For both of them. How much he wanted what was best for her. With that in mind, he couldn't bring himself to stop meddling. "I'm only speaking up because I care."

She felt a scary, exciting tightness in her throat. "Just how do you care, Garrett?"

"Well..." he trailed off haltingly. "There's always been a chemistry between us, dating way back when you were too young to know."

Shari slanted her gaze to the mirror behind the bar to conceal her sharp and uncontrolled reaction. Sure enough there were traces of her alter ego's cynicism scrunching her nose, tilting her mouth. Obviously, Garrett was primed to test the waters without wading in too deep.

Forever keeping his options open for Flame.

"I was very aware of how things were then," she assured him. "But going back doesn't serve today. In fact, it seems to me a roadblock, an excuse not to— Oh!" She'd smacked her stemmed glass down on the bar, causing the martini to slosh over the teak surface of the bar. "The wood—" Frantically she scanned for a towel. Finding one draped on a rod before the rows of bottles, she snatched it up and glided it over the damp wood surface. "Sorry."

His hand covered hers, slowing down the towel. "It's nothing."

"It's teak!" Her voice was an embarrassing squeak.

"So it is," he maintained calmly. "So what?"

"So let me clean it up."

"One swipe will do it." He guided her hand and the towel over the spill, then took her moistened fingertips to his mouth for a taste of crisp martini.

Electricity traveled the length of her arm, sending a sizzle through her veins. She shook visibly.

"Garrett..." Instinctively she tugged in protest. He held firm, sucking harder on her fingers. "Some men prefer their drink with an olive," she said weakly.

"Do you like this?" he demanded.

Her eyes closed, and she leaned against the bar. "Oh, yes..."

Garrett leisurely nibbled on her fingers, watching the way her lashes fluttered against her cheeks, the amatory slack of her mouth. Impulsively he caught her in the crook of his arm and hauled her close for a crushing kiss.

Caught by surprise, she popped open her eyes and locked onto his simmering gaze. If only he knew what he was doing to her, if only he understood this was by all rights a kind of foreplay, rather than just play. She couldn't help melting into him wantonly, taking chances she hadn't in her apartment kitchen.

He was slightly startled by the body contact but wasted no time wondering about it. The hand at her waist lowered to squeeze her bottom and his free hand palmed a breast.

They groaned in mutual pleasure.

There was no Dylan to interfere this time.

Shari's brain was ticking madly through her waves of

desire. If she let him go so far, she would be obligated to follow through. Already she could feel the hand crushing her skirt as though to lift the hem higher. The moment he invaded that hidden territory between her thighs, neither of them would be rational enough to stop. Within minutes he'd discover her secrets.

In the moments to come, she played catch-me-if-you-can with his hands, redirecting them, taming them. It was in plain contradiction with her moist and pliable mouth, which gave him the complete go sign. But even with her kisses she was holding back, letting him lead, have his way with her.

Surely he was out of his mind with confusion.

He began to kiss her temples, shifting to her ear. "Shari, I would never hurt you."

Her fingers lighted on his chest. "I know that."

"You drive me crazy with your modesty," he confided. "I swear there's a raging furnace running inside you. There has to be, with the heat between us."

Her eyes darted one way, then the other. "About Peters…"

"He knows when to stay out of the way."

Damn. He would be discreet.

He recaptured her mouth, moaning softly as he explored its velvet surface with his tongue. Her senses reeled. This was the side of Garrett she longed for, the hot and determined lover, sure of his own skills, anxious to fulfill.

As he flanked her limb for limb, she felt his rock-solid sex nudge her belly. Shari gasped with delight as he ground himself into her. Even with their layers of clothing, the friction was erotic, tempting. How frustrating to fully understand what they were missing. Garrett was at least spared that.

There was no misreading her signals, Garrett silently

rejoiced. Shari was softening with his advances. He tore his mouth from hers, branding her cheek, her throat. When she tipped her head back to welcome him, he put his lips on the nub of her breast, outlined so enticingly against the bodice of her dress. Careful not to moisten the cotton fabric, he nibbled at the hard circle of skin underneath. The best way to keep the dress neat would be to remove it. But was she ready for that? She was confident, bold.

Perhaps she wasn't as shy and inexperienced as he thought. Perhaps with further coaxing she'd let the dress go.

Again Shari felt his hands at her hemline, fabric bunching as his fingertips glided up the backs of her bare thighs with a feathery tickle. She didn't stop him this time. Instead she joyously anticipated his huge palms cupping her satin-clad bottom and responded with a soft cry as a flood of liquid desire dampened that satin.

It was with breathless reluctance that she pushed him off her. "I'm not ready for this. Sorry."

His breathing was labored, too, as he righted himself. "That's all right." There wasn't much conviction in his tone, but an affectionate smile was on the rise. "I think I understand."

"Yeah?" She already didn't like the knowing light in his eye.

"You're a tease still testing your wings." He tapped her nose. "Which is understandable, with your background."

"Meaning?"

"It's plain to see you've been cooped up in that shop too long with Dylan. He guards you so closely, you probably haven't had the chance to explore sexual boundaries."

"That's how you see it. I'm inexperienced."

"I don't think you completely understand what you can do to a man," he said huskily. "What you just did to me."

"What did I do?"

"Near drove me to the edge." He wagged a chiding finger at her. "Better watch that in the future. You may lead the wrong guy on one of these days and he's going to expect the works."

Garrett's message sank in slowly. He was actually insinuating she was a novice at lovemaking—and at the same time implying he was a master of the art! She could have gleefully slapped away his superior smile. Even stronger was the temptation to reach below the belt and give him the surprise of his privileged life.

Fortunately, reason broke through. Garrett had the talent to get her emotions roiling like no one else. She could weather her annoyance if she made an effort to calm herself.

It was definitely time to break, move to opposite corners for some time-out. She gathered her wits the best she could. "I really should be going."

Distress clouded his features. "But there are things I hoped to talk over."

Sure, like the details for the big bash that was supposed to drive Flame out into the open. Shari was too wrung out today to go on playing the little mascot who ran the coffee shop. She eased out from behind the bar with one eye on her purse. "I don't think you're in any frame of mind to see the real me, Garrett. For the record, your little speech here was nothing but a crock." She stood in the middle of the living room, hoping he'd demand her version and insist she reveal herself. But that wasn't to be. Instead of melting down, he froze up completely.

With a new air of formality he escorted her to the

street, hailed a cab and paid the driver in advance. Shari realized he would appear the perfect gentleman to any passerby, collected, relaxed. Removed. Despite her anger, it stung her that he could frost over so easily, function smoothly with a stiff upper lip. Guess that took years of practice under the finest tutelage. On her street, people just flipped out with nerve and passion.

He kept up the facade until the end as he opened the back door of the cab, briskly stepping back. Nervous, letdown, self-conscious, she lunged into the back seat of the yellow vehicle, slamming the door closed. She turned away as the cab lurched into traffic.

When Garrett reentered his apartment, Peters was conspicuous once again, sitting in the master bedroom sorting socks.

"You're back, sir. Everything go well?"

"I've just been rejected," he confided with amazement.

"Oh?"

"Yes! By an inexperienced minxy mouse. At least I think that's what she is."

Peters's narrow features glimmered with amusement. "If you don't mind my saying, I have trouble pinning the description of your gangly childhood tagalong to the lady who just swept out of here."

Garrett paced near the bed where Peters sat, his tone and expression razor sharp. "Meaning?"

"That to the objective eye, Shari Johnson is a real looker full of pizzazz."

"Hmm…" Garrett tapped his chin, giving the observation its due. "It's true, I am having a tough time figuring her game. Just when I think she's quite ordinary like the old days, I see hints of something extra. For example, she evolved into the dish you saw this afternoon by surprise. Once we got dancing, she began to transform herself, until I simply couldn't resist making a move. There seems to be a pattern brewing. She often seems plain when I approach her, but quickly gets all pink and lovely and irresistible."

"Some women have complex personalities. To attract a particular man, sometimes a woman will experiment."

Garrett's profile hardened with pride. "I've made my interest clear enough. Nothing I do seems right."

"These things can take time and calculation."

"I think a huge part of the problem is that she's had limited chances at love play, what with her busy lifestyle and protective brother. My advances seem to make her edgy." Garrett threw his arms up in despair. "But did she appreciate my understanding on that score? No! Seems I just can't win."

With a soft chuckle Peters rose from the mattress with a stack of sorted socks and advanced to the dresser. "No woman, no matter how green, wants the fact pointed out to her."

Scalded but intrigued, Garrett trailed along, opening the top dresser drawer for the other man. "I was only trying to put her at ease. We're talking about the String Bean, for God's sake."

"My guess is that Shari is frustrated with that old image."

"Oh. Well, it's true that she doesn't like her old nickname. But it's hard to get out of the spirit of it all, that she's the little mascot."

Peters laid the socks out in order of color. "And then there's the other stumbling block you have."

"Which is?"

"The social barrier."

"But I try not to let that get in the way."

"Ah, but it's bigger than the two of you. Your mother's

involved and she magnifies those barriers. I've fallen victim to her myself enough to spot the signs."

"Shari readily admitted as much just today," Garrett conceded. "It isn't just my mother's involvement, but her brother's, too. She's very concerned that Gwen has the capacity to hurt Dylan."

"Old wounds, I'm sure, like the nickname."

"Now I'm more confused than ever about Shari's feelings."

"That suggests to me that you don't really know her well enough for second guesses about sex or anything else. Not yet." Peters smiled faintly.

"I have the suspicion that getting to know that one will take more effort than all my other relationships combined."

"Yes. Still waters and all that."

Garrett sighed. "She runs deep all right."

"But it is worth it."

"A man could drown on this mission," Garrett complained.

"If you want someone to talk you out of chasing Miss Johnson, I suggest your mother." Peters pushed the drawer closed with a grin. "I, on the other hand, have many bachelorhood memories of treading similar dangerous waters. Sometimes, when I'm doing a tedious chore, I think back very fondly on those days in the drink."

Garrett rubbed his hands together, tipping his dark head closer to Peters. "So, uh, any of these memories include your lovely wife?"

"As a matter of fact they do. Nothing more exciting in this whole world than misbehaving with the right woman. Naughty and nice, the best of them are. An intriguing blend of naughty and nice."

"But can the String Bean be naughty enough?"

Peters shook his head, his bald spot catching the light. "You will have to leave behind all those old images if you hope to survive this battle of the sexes. The Miss Johnson of today is a mature available female with mysteries to uncover. A worthy opponent. Viewing her as less will only set you back."

Garrett's pride was quickly at a tug-of-war with the idea that Shari had the capacity to toy with him, conceal things from him. The guys always had the upper hand with her. He enjoyed having the upper hand as much as Dylan did.

Still, she did have the capacity to turn him on spontaneously, unexpectedly.

But even at her naughtiest, it was difficult to imagine that Shari could burn as hot as Flame.

If only he hadn't been scorched by Flame in the first place. But if he hadn't gone through with the auction, he might never have stepped foot back into the Beanery and rediscovered Shari. The circle of life went round and round the center core of the coffee shop, with Shari and Flame rotating in the same orbit.

Garrett was quite sure he could love Shari thoroughly if he made a commitment. But he wanted to settle things with Flame first, get her out of his system completely. If possible...

Perhaps this chill between him and Shari was a good thing for now. He'd keep his distance until the Club Wed party at Spotlight Academy. Hopefully his one-night stand would show up for a rematch, give him the chance to sort out his feelings properly.

"WHERE THE HELL HAVE YOU BEEN until this hour?"

Dylan was startled by the chastisement. Shari generally minded her own business. But sure enough he turned to find her hanging out the doorway of her apartment dressed in her pink terry robe, glaring at him as he tried to unlock his abode.

"What are you doing up, anyway?" he shot back. With that he barged inside his door. Shari was on his heels, switching on lights. The spacious place was always comforting to them both, pretty much as their folks left it, save for the mess. As shipshape as Dylan kept the Beanery, his personal space was always a cluttered disaster.

Dylan tossed his keys on an end table and ran a hand through his wavy blond hair. "Aw, Shari, can't this wait until the morning?"

She poked an accusatory finger at him. "You are actually wearing a bonafide tie."

"Why sure," he said calmly. "So?"

"So—you're the clip-on king!"

"Not always."

She marched up to flick the strip of fabric with her fingers. Amazingly, it had the feel of silk. "Not that it especially matches the plaid in your shirt," she surmised critically, "but the knot is suspiciously neat."

"Well, Gwen redid the knot for me," he admitted. He wasted no time ambling over to an overstuffed orange chair in the living room, loosening the knot in question as he sat down.

Shari cried out in horror. "You were with Gwen McNamara all this time?"

"Well, you took off with Garrett."

"To conduct business at the Spotlight Academy."

"Which went very well, I hear."

Shari stood over him in her flowing pink robe with hands on her hips. "How?"

"Gwen and I dropped in at Garrett's after dinner."

"You dined with her?"

"At the River Cafe. They sure have a swell piano

there." He cocked his fair head in a dreamer's pose, one Shari well recognized. "I wonder if we should have a piano."

"No way. Our expenses are already plenty high."

"You are entirely too weird about the remodeling. Even Garrett and Gwen think so."

The very idea that they would discuss her so freely made her boil all the more. "Dylan, let's back up here. What were you doing with that dragon of a mother in the first place?"

"Oh, cut me some slack. You know how much I miss Mom. And Gwen was saying all the right mom things, like how's your diet and do you have a decent laundry—cool codependent stuff like that. Why, she even said a couple of kind things about you, like how you didn't go to fat after puberty."

Shari rolled her eyes. "Dylan, please don't expect anything real and fulfilling from this woman."

"But I like being fussed over, mothered. Even if it isn't strictly on the level."

"Yes, you would." Deflated, Shari sank down on his chair's matching ottoman. Seconds later she felt her brother's hand stroking her hair.

"Gwen can be real nice when she puts her mind to it. And she has so much attention to give. Poor Garrett seems mighty relieved to have a fellow recipient. And it could grow into something even better. She's taken a keen interest in our remodeling. Wants to confer with Kyle Saunders personally, make sure our vision blends perfectly with his."

"Dylan, you're setting yourself up for a letdown here. The McNamaras, Elite House—they're two corporations too rich for our blood."

"It's all reasonable, Shari."

She gripped the edges of the ottoman, remembering

how coolly Garrett had dismissed her on the street after their quarrel, how insignificant she'd felt. He was trained in the art of rejection. "No, you're thinking too swank."

"But we can afford it now. You're just used to keeping the belt tight because the folks always did. We're covered, thanks to the inheritance. I just feel our business can reach new heights with the McNamaras behind us."

"Wake up, Dylan! There's nothing but the lure of a fantasy woman holding them here right now! How durable a bond can that be?"

Shari instantly realized that her anger was way out of line. Contrite, she swiveled round on her seat and patted the knee of his crisp new navy trousers. "Oh hell, maybe I'm overly defensive because I don't want us hurt."

"Give me some credit, sis. I know it's possible that once the fanfare dies down, Garrett might tire of us, decide he's slumming."

Her lips thinned. "Exactly."

"Still, I've chosen to look on the positive side. All the old team is so grateful to have him back, and they're giving me credit for it. Jimbo's already consulting Garrett about some stocks for his kid's college fund, and Mark's looking to improve his retirement plan. To us guys, this seems like the jump start to a bigger and better friendship."

"Those are the kinds of bonds that really do mean something," she agreed.

"Having the best remodeling job for the shop will make my new and improved life just about perfect."

"I will let you know what decorator I want!"

"If we make it good, this could become the romance capital of Manhattan."

"For someone who refuses to use Club Wed himself, you sure are a crazy romantic."

Dylan's expression grew wily all of a sudden. "Speaking of crazy, Garrett was full of personal questions tonight about you."

Shari gasped. "Such as?"

"Oh, what you've been up to since school, if you have a problem handling your money."

"Why would he care?"

"Like me, he's beginning to wonder why you don't want to hire Elite House and get the job done." Dylan chuckled. "He has the idea that you may have squandered your money. Imagine that, you of all people! Even wondered if you're an Atlantic City gambler."

She balled her fists. The nerve. The gall. First he assumed she was sexually inexperienced because she'd been hesitating on the make, and now he assumed she'd gambled the money away because she'd been hesitating on the remodeling.

Dylan stopped laughing in the face of her rage. "He isn't right, is he? You didn't lose your fortune playing roulette or something?"

"Don't be stupid," she snapped. "When do I ever get away on my own?"

Dylan grinned. "Right. Told him you weren't the type to mess up." But there was a wary gleam in his eye that Shari knew was bound to cause some trouble. Dylan was going to be on her case more than ever.

11

"THE HAIR'S ABSOLUTE HEAVEN again! Up to Flame's high standards." Shari sat up straighter in Magda's all-purpose barber's chair, mere hours before the Club Wed party. Magda was hovering chairside with her hairdresser friend Clinton, who had for a second time managed to transform Shari's buttery mane into a coppery crown of splendor.

The threesome stared at Shari's reflection in the giant mirror over the well-stocked vanity table, making appreciative sounds. The transformation was incredible.

Shari always enjoyed her visits to Magda's off-Broadway studio apartment. It was as eccentric as she was, chock-full of props and souvenirs from her numerous stage performances. This multipurpose bedroom-beauty-salon was the largest room of the three, equipped with terrific lighting and every cosmetic known to civilized man.

The perfect place to create a siren princess.

"It's your turn at bat, Mags," Shari coaxed. "Trowel on my new face. Make it even better than the last time."

Magda began to dab foundation on Shari's forehead with a sponge and was soon making disapproving sounds. "If you want magical results, you will have to work with me from the inside out."

"What do you mean?"

"That much of your glow the last time was from natural excitement."

"I'm excited."

"Come now, Shari. You're aroused with anger for your lover, not amour."

"Only natural, after the high-handed way Garrett's treated me. Thinks I'm a rookie lover—hah!"

"He's been intrigued with both you and Flame, and naturally he's comparing your charms. Compared to your alter ego, you would seem tame."

"That's another thing, the way he's been stringing me along when he can't forget *her*."

Magda cackled. "I'd like to be around when you challenge that point of logic."

"I don't intend to. After tonight, Flame will be gone for good."

"And then you'll have him all to yourself," Clinton deduced.

"Will I really?" Shari seethed. "He's steered clear of me for nearly two weeks, since our tussle at his apartment."

Magda patted foundation onto Shari's tight jaw. "Don't even think about tomorrow's losses tonight. Focus solely on this role, on letting Garrett down easy."

"He doesn't deserve easy anymore." Shari squirmed under the plastic cloak cinched at her neck. "Did I mention that he suspects I have a gambling problem on top of being frigid?"

Magda made a tsking sound. "At least a dozen times."

"I was speaking to Clinton," Shari said with a sniff.

With an apologetic wince, the slender, bearded man fluffed some hair over Shari's ear with a metal pick. "You haven't mentioned it for a whole hour or so."

"Oh. Well, it certainly bears repeating hourly."

"Come now, it's time you take over the Flame identity entirely," Magda advised, pressing her hand to her diaphragm. "Speak from down here. And quit knocking the lover of your dreams."

"What if I'm not ready to be the light and playful Flame yet?"

"I will stick this sponge in your mouth until you are."

Shari sank down in the chair. "I'm ready, I'm ready."

Tracy came bursting into the room moments later, her long black mane flying. "That was Dylan on the telephone. He's going nuts looking for Shari."

Magda frowned. "What did you tell him?"

"That she was meeting an old friend in Jersey for dinner."

Shari groaned. "I never go to Jersey. That's an awful alibi."

Tracy clapped a hand to her cheek. "Sorry, but we didn't discuss your cover story. And I was thinking of Jersey because I just visited my aunt there."

"But he'll think I'm in Atlantic City gambling!" Shari lamented.

"That cannot be helped anymore," Magda snapped practically. "And it is the lesser of two extremes. Better that big brother thinks you're hooked on keno than hooked on Garrett."

Even Shari had no argument for that.

"Oh, yes, Magda," Tracy added, moving closer to the chair. "Your actor pal called."

Magda wasn't so practical about this message. "But I have dozens!"

"I mean the guy from the rep company," Tracy said patiently, "the one who's playing chauffeur. He's in the limo and on his way across town."

Shari brightened with that news flash. "Thank heavens. And thanks again to you, Mags, for setting up my transport. I don't dare spend too much time at Lily Fleur's. The odds of getting busted this time will be highly increased with Dylan and the club members floating around."

"Don't mention it," Magda cooed, patting her cloaked shoulder. "Jerome is an old and dear friend who owes me several favors. He's ready and able to drive you and Garrett around on a private tour of the city or peel out with only you for a quick getaway. A rap on the dividing window is all it will take to bring him to your beck and call."

"Perfect."

"The whole thing shouldn't take long, though, since you plan to dump Garrett as quickly and painlessly as possible."

"I told you—"

"You will stick to the original plan of letting him down easy, my girl," Magda lectured. "*Capisc'?*"

Shari tipped her nose with a haughty sniff. "Being that he's dumped Shari so heartlessly, Flame's considering another round of lovin' em and leavin' em. She is leaving that option wide open."

LILY FLEUR GREETED the tuxedoed Garrett and Dylan at the entrance to her studio at precisely seven o'clock. Detaining them, she scanned the welcome table for their badges. Each badge had a spring-loaded clip, which she attached to their jacket pockets. "There now, you're labeled properly. Come along inside, see how the place fares."

The men exchanged approving looks as they strolled into the studio. The lights were dimmed, setting off the polished wood flooring. The music was muted, controlled by a deejay stationed at the entertainment center. Silver cutouts of stars and planets hung over the tall windows.

"Very nice," Dylan noted. "Not too extravagant."

"Gwen tried to go overboard, but I told her this wasn't one of your regular occasions. Spotlight is a modest establishment."

"Just the right touch for our members," Dylan assured.

Garrett took his old instructor's plump hand. Her mint chiffon dress billowed as he pulled her into a close hold. "Lily, you're still a wonder."

"And I still like to lead." With that, Lily did a quick three-step chassé, which Garrett automatically followed. Laughing, they broke apart.

Dylan rubbed his hands together, further formulating details of his plan B. "I still think the moment Flame steps into the room, we should bolt the door."

"And lose my lease over a fire code?" Lily reprimanded. "Think again."

"Yes, ma'am." Dylan shrank a bit, as he used to when Lily scolded him for chewing gum in class.

"No use of force would be right," Garrett remarked wistfully, shoving his hands in his pant pockets. "If Flame shows, I should be able to keep her here on my own. If not, I guess I don't deserve her." Not sure what he deserved drew his thoughts to Shari. He asked Dylan about her.

"Tracy claims that she's in Jersey visiting some old friend," Dylan replied flatly. "But we know better."

Garrett flashed him a distracted frown. "We do?"

"Sure. Your suspicion about her having a gambling problem makes more sense by the minute."

As grateful as Garrett was to have Shari out of the way for this possible reunion with his sexy bidder, he was uncomfortable about the trouble he'd stirred up about Shari's finances. "I think you should slow down, not jump to any conclusions."

"Yeah? I'll have you know I probed into her finances

this week and there's a huge chunk of money missing from her savings."

Garrett growled in dismay. "I didn't mean for you to go that far."

"Don't misunderstand, I thank you for the tip."

Garrett raised his palms. "Please don't, buddy. You're beyond my limits."

"Don't be so modest. I figure together we have a much better chance of raising little sister right." Dylan raked a hand through his wavy blond hair. "Don't you see? Your insight will no doubt be invaluable—make up where I've been lacking."

Garrett reddened in discomfort as he thought back to the strain his insightful observations had already put on his relationship with Shari. "Have to warn you, Dylan, little sister sees herself as capable of handling her own affairs."

Dylan wasn't even listening. "Just can't believe I missed the signs of addiction. Wonder what they were..."

Garrett slapped him on the back, noting that there were Club Wed members streaming into the studio. "Let's concentrate on your guests."

"Yeah, fixing you up is the night's priority."

"It wouldn't hurt for you to do a little flirting tonight yourself."

"I never mess with the customers," Dylan stated adamantly.

Garrett gave him a shove. "Well, maybe it's a policy that needs remodeling along with the decor. C'mon."

She arrived exactly forty-five minutes into the party.

Garrett was standing near the deejay, making small talk about the area's best gyms. He'd danced with a few club members to be sociable, but his eyes rarely strayed far from the sliding steel door where Lily was greeting newcomers.

He wanted to be the first to see her and he was. Dressed to squeeze men's hearts all over again in her red beaded gown, she breezed by the preoccupied Lily without the standard-issue name tag.

It was clearly understood. She was above such pretense and expected. Had she come to figure that this whole party was a trap for her?

If so, she was behaving nothing like prey. She glided in owning the place. Owning him. One look into those hypnotic aquamarine eyes and he was a goner. They were just as vivid in color as he remembered. In fact, his memories in general had been amazingly accurate. Flame was indeed larger than life. A fantasy lover. A goddess. A dream.

The music began to play. Garrett had told the deejay in advance exactly what he wanted if this moment ever arrived: a searing tango, giving their bodies an appropriate excuse to touch.

She came to him, her face full of triumph and mischief. "You came...."

"This is no time for talk," she said throatily, easing up against him.

It was magic all over again, the way they swayed with incredible timing and grace, their forms a true and snug fit. The flow of their dance reminded Garrett of time spent with Shari on this very floor, the curve of her body, her seemingly psychic ability to sway and turn on cue.

But Shari was best forgotten for the moment. He owed Flame his undivided attention, if only for the night.

Once and for all he would get her out of his system or end up incinerated.

"Good evening, Dylan."

"Gwen." Dylan's grin broadened and he broke away

from a small gathering near the check-in table to greet the dowager, who was dressed in a sleeveless black sheath with bolero jacket.

"How much potential you hold in a tuxedo."

Dylan's smile wavered, sure that Shari would consider that a backhanded compliment. But who was handling whom here, when it came right down to it? The McNamaras were on his turf, enjoying his hospitality, complimenting his threads. When he got the chance he'd have to tutor his sister on exactly how to mingle and conquer the upper-class crowd.

Gwen clasped her jeweled hands together. "Dare I hope?"

"Our plan B worked," Dylan reported, puffing with pride. "She's here."

With a small gasp of pleasure, Gwen tugged Dylan across the entry area for a peek at the dance floor. She sagged against the door frame. "Oh, yes. Just the same. Feminine perfection. Grace in fashion and style." Her face was radiant as she stared up at Dylan. "And look at them glide as one. Sheer poetry in motion."

"That she is. Garrett's one lucky man."

"How long has she been here?"

Dylan shrugged beneath his tailored jacket. "About fifteen minutes. Even I haven't gotten an introduction yet. Several other people have tried to cut in with no luck, so I've been keeping my distance."

"You must get me out on the floor to greet her."

He sagged like a sulky teen. "But the waltz is one of my weaker dances."

"Come now, dear. Do it for me."

Dear? Dylan glowed, holding his arms out to her. "May I have the honor?"

Garrett immediately noticed the odd couple waltzing into range. And Flame noticed his strained expression.

"Catch something in your zipper?" she teased.

"Very funny." He guided her into a sweeping turn, tipping his raven head to the left. "I know you can't begin to appreciate the threat of the May-December partners coming alongside us, but trust my instincts to flee."

Flame worked to keep a bland expression as her aquamarine peepers landed on Dylan gingerly twirling Gwen McNamara around like a bone-china vase. She was half tempted to step out of character and wallop her brother Shari-style.

Per Gwen's direction, Dylan was obviously trying to edge in on the other couple without cracking his bony partner in two. Garrett was deliberately making it a challenge with some snappy maneuvers.

Anyone rarely got the best of Gwen McNamara, though. With a smooth transition, she was leading her beefy, towering partner and sending a warning look to her son. Once in range she cooed out in salutation, "Flame darling, welcome."

Shari nodded and smiled as Garrett locked them into a holding pattern beside the other couple. Dylan wouldn't recognize her even at his close proximity. Of course he wouldn't. Not only was she artfully made-up, but his mind's eye forever held an image of Shari at thirteen, with braces and braids and freckles. Dylan's mulish determination to keep her the chaste child was, for once, a blessing. Anything his unconscious might sense, his narrow-minded mentality would quickly dismiss.

Because of the loud music, Gwen overexaggerated her words. "We must all get together for a nice chat."

Shari took delight in emulating Gwen's nose crunching and lip pursing before Garrett whisked her off again.

"You don't want to chat with Mother, do you?"

When pigs fly and the rivers run dry. "Sorry, no."

"But you did want to see me again."

"Let's say you're more persistent than I ever dreamed possible."

The music was dying away, so Flame cleverly pulled Garrett out of sight into a small throng of club members. Her heart sank as she noted that Gwen was intently looking for them and well on the way to watch over the only official exit.

Garrett noticed Gwen's move, as well. "Have you figured out that this whole party was contrived to flush you out of hiding? Trap you here for my personal enjoyment?"

Flame laughed huskily. "Calling it Blame the Flame personalized the event. Very clever, as you know how much I enjoy games."

He couldn't conceal his impatience any longer. "Please tell me why you have been avoiding me."

She pressed a finger to his lips. "Not here. I have a limo downstairs, waiting for us."

His handsome face lighted. "Ah, another game."

"Yes, I suppose." Shari was feeling a rush of delicious power. How much he was enjoying this reunion. There was the promise of sex in his silvered eyes. He was thinking sex, tasting sex. Fully expecting sex.

How convenient if Flame *was* in the mood for sex.

Renewing their passion tonight would not be the sensible thing to do. It would only make it harder for Shari to step in and take over the relationship if she was given another opportunity. But Flame was feeling drunk on power right now, controlling the vital Garrett McNamara body and soul, knowing so much about him while he knew precious little about her.

She would press him to the limit now to make up for all the trouble he'd given her as Shari; the inferences that she was a naive tease, that she was a lousy money manager. It would be sweet release to make love to him, sweet revenge to have sex with him.

Heat centered at the apex between her thighs. It was with sheer daring and rebellion that she told him she was once again wearing no underpants.

He took the news with lusty anticipation. "I'd like to see you prove it—if we can manage to get away."

She tipped her fiery head toward the fire escape. "I'm leaving this way. I'll leave your escape to you."

"Where will we meet?"

"There's only one limo downstairs, I'm sure."

"Make that two, if I know my mother."

She'd forgotten about that possibility. Keeping her savvy, she flicked his chin with a long false nail. "If you stumble into the wrong back seat, pet, you don't deserve to pass go."

His expression hardened. "I don't know that I like being called your pet."

"Ah, but it's exactly what you are." With a flirty wink she eased out the already open window and onto the steel platform.

Amazingly, Magda and Tracy came up on either side of Garrett just then.

"So that's the lady that's been turning the shop upside down," Magda purred.

"Very attractive," Tracy noted, gazing out the window. "Though I don't think she's very good with ladders."

Garrett spun around to the pane. "Is she all right?"

"Sure, nearly all the way down now."

"So did either of you recognize her?" Garrett demanded impatiently.

"I don't believe so," Magda declared slowly. "Did she admit to being a member of the club?"

"She left me a note, she must be a member," Garrett challenged.

"Does it matter in the long run?" Tracy asked.

"It matters," Garrett snapped. "She's leading me around by the nose and I still know nothing about her! If only I had something to go on, a way to turn the tables."

Magda and Tracy stared at him helplessly.

Dylan sidled up to the group, giving Garrett a friendly nudge. "Hey, is she ever foxy!"

"But do you know her, Dylan?" Tracy couldn't resist asking for her and Magda's amusement.

Dylan stared into the middle of the floor, where dancers were attempting the fox-trot. "I don't think so."

Tracy folded her arms across the bodice of her bright polka-dot dress, too tickled to meet Magda's eye. "This is just the craziest set of circumstances, no one being able to pin this woman down."

"I intend to give this investigation another shot right now," Garrett asserted, smoothing his neat bow tie.

Dylan looked worried. "Gwen's determined to horn in."

"So be a good surrogate brother and distract her for me." With a grimace Garrett marched toward the sliding steel door.

Gwen hooked arms with her son as he passed by the table holding the badges. "Where are you going?"

"Out for a breath of fresh air."

"But what about—"

"It'll be up to you to keep her company while I'm out," Garrett murmured urgently, glancing at Dylan, who nodded in agreement.

Gwen swelled with power. "Where is she?"

"Probably where most girls end up after a while."

Gwen lifted a finger in understanding. "Ah, the rest room."

"If you say so." Kissing his mother's cheek, he left.

There were two black stretch limos at the curb as Garrett expected, each sporting a uniformed driver. There was no problem telling them apart. The chauffeur leaning against the family putt-putt smoking a cigarette was a familiar and capable employee. He straightened to full attention at the sight of Garrett and was openly shocked when he passed him right on by for the other vehicle. The second driver was not at all alarmed by his arrival and swept open the back door for him.

"Care for a spin around the park?" Flame's voice was liquid velvet in the cool, quiet night.

Garrett slid into the car like a hungry panther. It wasn't until the door was closed firmly behind him that he realized Flame was in the nude.

12

"I WANT TO OWN YOU TONIGHT, Garrett. Do you want that?"

He sat back on the seat across from her, a lazy, confident smile playing around the corners of his mouth. There was nothing he'd like better. But admitting it now would, well, spoil the game. "Care to negotiate those terms?"

"No."

He sat on his hands, fearing he couldn't keep them still any other way. She actually was naked. Waiting for him without a stitch. Her nerve was incredible. Her attitude careless. Her will steely. This was crazy and he was loving every minute.

"At least I deserve some answers," he reprimanded. "Have you any idea what I've been going through searching for you?"

"Yes," she murmured dryly, "and it wasn't exactly a stretch on the rack."

"That's exactly what if felt like! So, you must have friends in the coffee shop who tell you things, then?"

"I spend time there myself."

"What!"

He watched her cross one long leg over the other. The body was perfect, just as he remembered. Lean flared hips, small full breasts. He ached with desire.

They were moving in traffic now, each poised electrically on a separate leather upholstered seat in the long, luxurious automobile. A glimmer of streetlights shone through the tinted windows, illuminating her profile as she turned from him. Her skin was flawless, the bare column of her throat a creamy ivory where the stage makeup stopped.

It was an effort to catch his breath, form a clear sentence. The need to know things spurred him on, though. "Do you mean to tell me that you walk among the patrons unrecognizable?"

"Unnoticed," she corrected. "I roam freely in complete anonymity."

"Really…" He assessed her again, with no glimmer of recognition. "You must think me a bumbling fool right about now."

"Not at all. I am just too clever."

"So, did you mean what you said in the note?"

"Yes. We would never work in the real world. Trust me."

"Then maybe you shouldn't have come tonight at all."

"But you wanted closure."

"How do you know that detail?"

"I listen, I see things. It's easy when you're unnoticed."

This was incredible. She'd been close enough to eavesdrop on him and he didn't know it. How could he have blundered so? "So I get closure," he reasoned. "What do you get out of all this trouble?"

She quivered openly, uncrossing her legs. "Passion. You're my best lover ever."

He swelled with pride. That went far to appease his bungling.

"Oblige me, Garrett. Give me control. It's a harmless desire, really. And lots of fun the last time."

"Guess you did call all the shots that night, didn't you?"

"And it was a huge success." Her painted mouth curved as she crawled onto his seat, into his lap.

His groan was labored as she began to work open his tie, his shirt. "If we do this, I want to see you again. To talk."

Her breath was hot against his ear. "No."

Pure lust was crowding his system, short-circuiting his powers of logic. With hands clamped to her wrists, he thought fast, spoke fast. "I deserve to know who you are. I don't like the idea of you watching over me at the coffee shop, my having no clue."

"Forget this whole thing." Her coppery hair flew as she shook her head, trying to wrench off him. He held her still on his thighs with a chuckle.

"Simmer down. I'll make the terms fair. Say, for instance, if one day I were to spot you on the premises of the Beanery, you would admit to who you are and let me be in control for a change. Okay?"

She was dead-bang certain he'd never get it. The twinkle in those startling aqua eyes left no doubt. "Very well. Now let go of my wrists."

He did. There was no choice really. He wanted her badly, in a blind, thoughtless heat. She was the sexiest woman on the planet, with her secrets and ploys. Driving himself inside her was suddenly his only focus. He'd have promised her anything to get in there.

Straddling him, she continued to open the layers of his formal attire. He began to touch her while she worked, cupping her bottom, slipping his long fingers between her parted thighs, touching her moist opening. She gasped with pleasure, already wet for him; she probably had been that way all night long as they'd danced and teased and made proper conversation in public.

Leading him along by a long, invisible leash was a huge turn-on to her.

She was unbuckling his belt now, yanking at his zipper. It was certain that she had no intention of stripping him down, just peeling him open.

He rubbed her slick flesh with feathery fingertips, never going too deep. He had to be causing her a hot and exquisite torture by the swelling of her skin, the hoarseness of her breathing.

She hoped to indulge and forget. He hoped to brand her for good.

Having exposed enough of his hair-roughened skin to satisfy her, she braced one hand on his shoulder and the other on his arousal. Ever so slowly she gave him the treatment he'd given her, grazing the pad of her thumb over and over the tip of his rigid flesh. Then, without warning, she took him into her mouth, tasting his salty velvet skin.

He sat back on the supple leather seat, allowing glorious sensations to ripple through him.

Then it was his turn to taste her. He pushed her back flat on the seat, parted her legs and made slow, exquisite love to her with his tongue.

The limo rolled on for miles as they explored each other's bodies all over again, moving from seat to seat, sending her discarded gown sliding, her evening bag and its contents toppling to the floor.

He finally came while on top of her along the rear seat. She'd come several times by then.

Garrett would have expected his lover to very casually slip back into her gown, giving him a show to remember, but she didn't. Modestly, almost dishearteningly, she dressed herself at a distance in the spacious vehicle. Getting his clothes back in order first, he began to retrieve the contents of her bag. She accepted it with a wan smile, then slithered back up to the front to rap on the dividing window to signal the driver.

Within ten minutes they were parked at curbside. Right outside his penthouse. The driver wasted no time opening the back door onto the sidewalk.

Garrett lingered in the car only a moment, vaguely puzzled by the sad glimmer new to those vivid gemstone eyes. "Thanks for not dumping me in SoHo," he said, brushing his lips against hers. "But you better know it's wrong to dump me this way at all."

She grazed his solid jaw with a long red fingertip. "Goodbye, sweet prince."

Having shared her every emotion for nearly two hours, Garrett couldn't help plugging into the forlornness of her farewell as he stood stock-still, watching the limo streak off into the night.

"YOU ACTUALLY MADE LOVE AGAIN?" Tracy's voice was a shriek as she and Magda settled back in the limo some time later. "I thought that was an empty threat."

"Oh, Shari." Magda shook her head woefully. "Love 'em and leave 'em is so painful a way to break up."

"It hurt me the most." Shari pushed the stiff metallic hair from her vision, fighting back the sniffles.

"How could you give in?"

"I was determined to control him one last time, one way or the other. And he has a way of seducing me through dance," Shari admitted. "Every time I'm in his arms I sort of pretend we're at his senior prom. There's something so sexy about that man in a tux. Before I knew it, I was telling him I wore no panties."

"Now it'll be forever before you can put the moves on him as Shari," Tracy retorted.

"He doesn't want a relationship with an ordinary shop girl anyway," Shari surmised sadly. "His brush off these past couple of weeks suggested that, and his giving in to Flame tonight seals things up tight. If he truly loved me, Shari, he would've said no to Flame."

"He has made no commitment to you because you've refused to let him close," Magda argued.

"Plan B did a lot to spoil my progress. Got Garrett fired up all over again."

Magda nodded humbly. "I know that I am partly to blame for encouraging the trap for Flame. It seemed harmless fun at first. There you were, mocking every pretense the McNamaras have. Gwen drooling all over the both of us."

Shari waved her off. "You already apologized for that. It's done. Besides, I'm ultimately to blame for this fiasco."

"The man is like a drug to you," Tracy sagely observed. "When your confidence is high you can't keep your hands off him."

Shari sat up a bit straighter. "Guess I'll have to get used to doing just that. I dumped him for good as Flame, and as far as he and his mother are concerned, I'm the little dope."

The threesome had made plans in advance to crash in Shari's apartment after the party to discuss the evening's events. Magda's actor friend had dropped them off a half block from the Beanery. Any subterfuge was for Dylan's benefit, of course. But it was highly unlikely he was back yet, having left the academy for a late snack with his new surrogate mom, Gwen. Once in the building, however, they remained cautious, taking the enclosed staircase leading up to the second-floor apartments in stockinged feet, tiptoeing down the hallway past his apartment door. At this rate he'd never catch them even if he was already snug in bed.

As they approached her door, Shari unclipped the clasp of her black evening bag and rummaged for her

Beanery key ring. She moved in ahead of Tracy and grabbed the doorknob. She was about to insert her key when the door flung open.

"Oh! Gee." Dylan swung the door open wide, stepping back. "Sorry, miss, I was expecting my—my—"

Shari put a palm on the center of his tattered white T-shirt and gave him a shove backward. Wide-eyed with confusion, he stumbled into the entry table holding her mail.

Tracy crowded in after Magda and secured the door.

Dylan continued to stare, pointing at the woman he knew as Flame. "What's going on? Why have you brought *her* here?"

Seeing this as a second-last hurrah, Shari played the scene for all it was worth, pinching and patting his cheek. "Ah, darling," she said gustily. "Your sister is an insignificant chit of a girl."

"Maybe so, but she's my insignificant chit—uh girl." Dylan cleared his throat, blushing as Magda and Tracy began to laugh. "This isn't funny. Shari's been gone for hours. I'm convinced she has a real gambling problem. What if she's stranded someplace?"

"I'm sure she will call you soon," Magda assured, steering him to the door. "In any case, we plan to wait right here for her."

"Well, okay." Dylan glared once more at his pal's fantasy lover, who was sauntering around as if she owned the place. "But let me know if you hear anything." With that Dylan exited.

Shari began to giggle along with her pair. "He hates not being taken seriously."

Tracy gestured toward the bathroom. "Go take your shower while we rustle up some snacks."

They were snacking on Chablis and crackers in the living room some forty minutes later when Shari gave Dylan a call. "Just wanted you to know I'm back," she said in her natural voice.

"Great, kid. I'll be right over."

"There's no—" She broke off as the dial tone buzzed in her ear. "He's coming over."

They heard a key in the lock moments later. Dylan rushed inside. "I'm so glad you're home safe and sound."

Shari shrugged. "Yeah. Ran out of chips. Oops, I mean I ran out of cards." She feigned embarrassment. "Guess I don't know what I mean."

"Hey, I could do with a snack." Dylan sank down on the sofa beside his sister and leaned into the coffee table holding the refreshments. "So, where'd she go?"

"Who?" Shari asked blankly.

He poured himself a generous glass of wine and took a healthy gulp. "Flame, dummy."

Shari sat back and tucked a leg under her body. "She wasn't here when I arrived."

"That's weird. I've been quietly reading at my place and didn't hear her go or you come." He looked accusingly at Tracy, then Magda. "And I've been thinking. Why would you bring that babe here in the first place? All of you claimed not to know her."

"We met her tonight," Magda explained airily over the rim of her stemmed glass.

Tracy nodded eagerly. "Liked her so much we wanted to introduce her to Shari."

Dylan frowned. "But she disappeared from the party about the time that Garrett did."

"She came back after you left with Gwen," Tracy replied. "All alone with nothing to do."

"Then why didn't she stay on here long enough to meet Shari?"

Shari sighed impatiently. "Obviously she isn't the stable kind. Who cares?"

"I do," he insisted. "What a looker!" He whistled.

"You think so?" Shari smiled meanly.

"Too bad you missed her, sis. The things you could learn about beauty and charisma."

"But you don't want me dolled up and full of nerve. You want me meek and behind the scenes."

"You could've stored up the tips for someday, though. I mean, the day will come when we part company. Eventually."

Shari reached out to the plate of crackers and brought two to his mouth. "Here, stuff these in before I go nuts—"

She stopped in midsentence as they both stared down at the bold false fingernails holding the crackers. Long scarlet talons that perfectly matched the beaded dress hanging in the bathroom. And then there were the colored contact lenses giving Shari's blue peepers an intriguing aqua hue. She'd forgotten to pop them out in favor of her glasses.

"No—no—no!" Dylan tried to speak up, choking on the dry crackers.

Shari plied him with wine. "Settle down. A showgirl gave—"

"Shut up! You think I'm stupid?"

She reared in affront. "Well, sure I do!"

"You are *Flame*," he stated firmly. Then in a smaller voice he said, "You aren't really, are you? *Are* you?"

Five minutes later Dylan was stretched out on the sofa with a cold compress on his forehead. "Oh, my. Oh, no." He groaned like a wounded animal.

Magda, seated on the cushion beside him, made a cooing sound. "It is all right, sweetie. Auntie Mags is here for you. Close your eyes."

"I need Shari. Come here, kid." He smiled as she hovered over the back of the sofa. "Take my hand."

Shari reached down to squeeze his cool, limp fingers. "This whole charade is nothing to concern yourself about."

His face pinched boyishly. "But the details of these past weeks keep rolling through my head."

"You can make it stop if you concentrate," she encouraged.

Dylan made an agonizing sound. "No, I can't. To think the woman that Garrett was bragging about—lusting after—was you! An innocent!"

She squeezed his hand harder. "I am not an innocent."

He squeezed back. "But you were."

"Was not."

Suddenly they were arm wrestling in midair, each trying to bring the other to mercy.

"Kiddies, stop this now." Magda clamped her hands on their arms and pried them loose. "The most important thing is that we put all this behind us. Shari got the sex she wanted—"

"He ruined you." Dylan made an agonizing sound.

"Did not!"

"In any case, Dylan," Magda continued sternly, "It will be up to you to hold tight to Shari's secret."

His chin jutted up stubbornly. "Why should I?"

"Because I'm asking you to," Shari scolded. "You've put your nose where it doesn't belong and now you'll have to live with the facts you dug up."

His head lolled on the sofa arm. "But why did you do it in the first place?"

"Because I've always loved him, that's why! Because I couldn't have him for real, that's why!" Shari broke away and paced.

Dylan balled a fist. "If I could think of some loophole to clean his clock on…"

Shari charged the back of the sofa again, shouting in his face. "Back off! I pulled the strings here. I paid for him. I—"

As an eerie light danced in his eyes, she slowly drew away. But he was quicker, grabbing her shoulder. "So that's where the money went. I've been so worked up about your deflowering that I forgot about the auction, the thirty-grand bid."

She smiled falsely. "At least I'm not a gambler like you thought. There's nothing I need curing of."

That last claim brought soft hoots from the sidelines.

Dylan, in the meantime, slackened his grip on her, looking blank and hollow.

Shari clucked sympathetically. "I'll get you another glass of wine."

"Make that a whiskey," he mumbled. "But only a half glass. We've gotta start cutting more corners around here."

GARRETT OCCASIONALLY MET with his business partners, Herb Crater and Ron Richtor, on the weekend and this particular Sunday was one of those occasions. The older men had insisted upon discussing a hot new account and descended upon Garrett's apartment early in the afternoon.

Garrett had been planning to escape his penthouse to avoid meeting up with his mother. Though she didn't care to admit Sundays were tough for her since her husband died, she would most likely continue her year-long habit of showing up at his place for solace. And last night's party at Lily's made her mission a double whammy. Gwen was sure to want details of his reunion with Flame.

As he sat at his dining room table with his colleagues, all sorts of possibilities for a more productive Sunday continued to roll through his mind. He'd considered going to the Beanery to see how everyone had survived the night. Oddly, the call he'd expected from Dylan concerning Shari's safe return never came. Maybe it was a good sign, as Dylan was entirely too protective—something he'd like to help Shari change in her brother. Clearly, she was tired of being hounded.

He half hoped to hear from her personally this morning. But that hadn't happened, either.

How badly he wanted to tell Shari that he was more than ready to throw himself on her mercy, admit that a fling for the sake of sex alone wasn't his style at all. It was high time they started to build on the emotion and spirit between them.

His door buzzer sounded about two o'clock, just as the meeting was winding down. Garrett left the summons to Peters.

"Ah, such a lovely sight. Men at work!" Gwen entered the dining room, unusually buoyant in a loose-fitting floral dress that softened her brittle image considerably. "Ronald, Herb, how nice to see you."

Their brows rose with surprise and approval as they returned salutations. Then their looks slanted to Gwen's companion, dressed in a similar dress of peach hue. "Fellows, I want you to meet my dear friend, Magda DuCharme."

"The stage's Magda DuCharme?" Herb queried, popping out of his chair like a cork from a bottle. "I'm honored. Thrilled. Wait until I tell Bernice."

Magda shook hands with both men. "We are off to dinner and a show later. Gwen just stopped by to tell her son something."

Garrett stood up stiffly, rounded the polished walnut

table. Taking his mother's arm, he guided her into the entryway.

Gwen was far more relaxed than he, and gently patted his arm. "Sorry to interrupt, dear."

"That's fine, Mother."

"Did you have a nice time last night?"

"Yes, I did."

"Good. And Flame?"

He hesitated. "This isn't the time or the place."

"Just give me the bottom line."

"We...decided things wouldn't work out after all."

"Oh." Disappointment flashed in her eyes. "I am so sorry—for you."

He smiled blandly. "I'll live."

"Is there anything I can do?"

Garrett patted the hand on his arm. "There is one thing."

"Name it. Please."

"Let the Johnsons down easy."

"Whatever do you mean?"

He scowled in frustration. "You know. The chase for my fantasy woman is over." She remained blank. "You chummed up to Dylan especially because of your mutual mission to find her, right?"

"Yes, that's true."

"In case you haven't noticed, Dylan's crazy about you."

"I've noticed." She rolled her eyes but didn't look especially displeased. "As it happens, he's sort of grown on me with his candid and unguarded ways. His interest in my mothering is so eager, so fresh. He isn't jaded the way you are, Garrett, having so many privileges handed you. He delights in the simplest pleasures, a buggy ride through the park, cocktails at the Coach House, a new tie from Brooks Brothers."

"Dylan doesn't wear ties."

"Not every day, not yet."

Garrett chuckled, hard enough to rock his chest. Then he took her hand and kissed it. "I love you, Mother."

"And I you." She swallowed hard. "About...what you said..."

"What did I say?"

She glanced away. "About my Sundays being hard because of Brent's passing."

"Yes?" he asked mildly, keeping hold of her hand.

"You just may have a point. I do like companionship on the weekend. As it happens, Magda does, too. It's always nice to discuss things with one's own generation without fear of being betrayed by one's own gossip mill. Having separate lives, she and I can do that."

"Excellent."

"She's introducing me to many people I've long idolized, too," Gwen confided excitedly. "I've grown quite fond of her."

Garrett took a deep breath. "So, in all this new openness and affection, do you think you'll find a place for Shari?"

Gwen faltered for the first time. "Well, I— Dylan tells me she might have a gambling problem!"

"I'm sure she doesn't, Mother."

Gwen took back her hand and poked him in the chest. "Is there something going on between you two that I should know about?"

"Maybe. I haven't been able to quite figure her out yet."

"Oh, son, figuring it out in advance takes the fun away."

"But you wouldn't hurt either of us, would you? By objecting, I mean."

"I will do my best, I promise." Gwen's flawless brow

wrinkled. "But she is a shop girl, darling. I will need time to extract you from the loving arms of our Flame."

Magda interrupted them just as Garrett was enveloping his mother in the kind of bear hug that threatened to muss her a little.

"I think we better be off," the actress confided, smoothing her turquoise-tinted hair. "My charms can be lethal to the most devoted married man if given in high doses."

Garrett walked them to the door. "Take care and have fun."

Magda touched his cheek. "And you, Garrett, just concentrate on the fun. Ta-ta."

13

SHARI BREEZED into the coffee shop around ten-thirty Monday morning to find Dylan seated at the chipped pumpkin counter with Kyle Saunders from the Elite House. They were just wrapping things up, it seemed, both men wearing full smiles as Dylan signed a document.

Kyle put the papers in his briefcase and stood to leave. Dylan stayed seated as he shook his hand. "Great, Kyle. We'll be seeing your people a week from tomorrow."

"Very good." With a nod to Shari, Kyle left.

Shari rounded the U-shaped serving station, dropped her purse in a bottom cabinet drawer and leaned across the counter into Dylan's face. "Are you out of your mind, calling that crook back in here?"

Dylan was unusually patient and amused. "His only crime is being the best. And I want the best for this place no matter what the cost."

"How did you swing the finances?"

"We have a new silent partner." Dylan gestured to a pay-phone alcove behind the living room grouping. Garrett, of all people, loomed in the archway with the receiver at his ear.

She cried out softly in alarm. "He's helping us? I thought you wanted to tear him apart for ruining me!"

Dylan waved dismissively. "I did consider roughing him up way back on Saturday night, but then I got to thinking that you were the one who shamelessly exploited him, lured him into your diabolical trap."

Shari eyed him carefully. "You really see that, Dylan?"

"Yup."

She whooped with glee. "Finally! You totally understand that I'm a capable woman with attitude and needs—"

"Nix the needs," he cut in sharply. "I don't want to even think about those. But the rest, I'm going to try and see. You're all grown up and there's no going back. I tried my best to keep you safe and centered and it left you suppressed, explosive."

"What a breakthrough. Hallelujah!"

He braced himself forward on an elbow, his features stern. "All I ask is the next time you have an itch, find a cheaper way to scratch it."

Shari craned her neck for another look at the oblivious Garrett and nervously drummed the counter with her fingers. "I wonder what possessed him to step in and help."

Dylan was matter-of-fact. "I suppose he's concerned about your gambling weakness."

"But I don't have one," she scoffed.

"So what is your official story about losing the money going to be, just for the record?"

She belligerently folded her arms across the front of her baggy green T-shirt. "None. That two-timer deserves no explanation."

"C'mon, Shari, what do I tell him if he asks me?"

"Play it stupid and naive…darling," she rasped in her best Flame imitation.

His hand came to rest on her collarbone "There are times I could smother you."

"You've already made that mistake," she sassed him with a grin. "Save up the rest of your ignorance for your own daughters."

He was horrified. "I'm not having kids. You're too

much trouble. Besides, I'm too busy being the second-best son Gwen ever had."

Garrett was startled to see Shari as he strode up the aisle toward the counter. But he was happy to see her. Never happier in fact.

He slid onto a stool as Dylan slid off one. "Everything set with Kyle?"

"Sure is." Dylan clapped his pal on the back and went to assist two lost-looking souls at the Club Wed station.

Garrett turned his attention across the counter to Shari, who was busily filling a napkin dispenser. "Missed you at the dance Saturday night," he said softly.

Her profile hardened. "Liar. I heard about your great time."

"So you recover from your adventure?"

She figured he meant her alleged gambling junket. If only he knew... Her stomach did a flip as she relived flashes of their tumbling exercises in the limo. The knowledge that she had indeed come to control him for a second time put her in a generous frame of mind. "I had loads of fun. Jersey's beautiful this time of year."

"In the dark?"

"Sure." She returned the napkin package to its shelf below the counter, then turned to face him with a smug smile. "By the way, congratulations. I hear you're in on the action."

It was his body's turn to react with a twinge. "Action?"

"Around here, I mean—picking up the financial slack."

"Oh, yes." He clasped his hands, taking a small, steadying breath. "Decent investment, I'd say."

"Surprised you think so, after steering clear of here for the past couple of weeks."

"You understand that full well," he retorted, looking from side to side to make sure no one was listening. "The way you fended me off back at my place. It was clear we both needed some space to think."

"Space to cool off in my case. You had a nerve suggesting I'm a tease."

Humor twinkled in his eyes. "Well, you are. I stand by that."

She curled her fist. "Believe it or not, mister, you don't know zip about me."

"I do want to know more, though." He paused, glancing around the shop as patrons began to gather. "Say, do you think we could continue this conversation up in your apartment?"

"Why would you want to speak to me at all?"

He hesitated. "Because I like teasers."

"I'm not— Oh, get lost. There's nothing more to say."

She tried to whirl back out of reach, but he leaned over the counter to snag her wrist. "Not so fast. Now that I'm an investor around here, I want to see only a spirit of goodwill among the staff. Nobody should see us bickering. This is supposed to be a fun place for lovebirds, remember?"

"I remember."

He loosened his grip on her. "Now, come on. I won't keep you long."

Shari muttered something unflattering under her breath, but grabbed the compact purse she'd just shoved into a drawer and marched to the door leading to the staircase. She clomped up the wooden stairs, keenly aware of his eyes on her swaying bottom. But he wouldn't really see her charms beneath her jeans and T-shirt, she knew. To him she'd always be the shapeless bean in comparison to Flame.

He opened the fire door on the landing, ushering her inside. "So, what did you do yesterday?" he asked casually. "Work?"

"No, I took the day off. I'm sure you've noticed the

odd college student waiting tables. When we're short-handed we call in even more."

They walked side by side down the hallway. "So you never left your apartment on Sunday for any reason?"

"What's it to you?"

Garrett shrugged beneath his tailored suit jacket, a sly crook to his mouth. "It might explain something that's been bothering me."

She wasn't about to give him the satisfaction of wondering what that tickler might be. Pausing at her apartment door, she dug into her purse for her Beanery key ring.

"About the financing, Shari—"

"Don't start in on me about what happened to my own money."

He deflected her ire with merriment. "I don't intend to. I was just going to say that I plan to be a very silent partner, leave the everyday details to you Johnsons."

"Good." Palming the key, she looked up at him. He somehow believed himself to have the upper hand and it made her nervous. "We could talk out here. We are alone, no impressionable customers in sight."

He rested a hand against the doorjamb, effectively crowding her with his large form. "I'd like to go inside if you don't mind."

"It's kind of a mess."

"No problem."

"Okay." With an unsteady shoulder twitch she tried to slip the key into the lock. Then tried again. For some reason, the key didn't fit.

But it was her key ring, wasn't it? Shari stared up into Garrett's handsome face, alight with mischief, then down at the green plastic disk bearing the name of the shop. She hadn't noticed how worn it was this morning when she'd hurriedly transferred it from her evening bag to her work handbag. Or how it was flecked with pink nail polish.

Slowly, she thought things through. The answer was startling, making her a little dizzy.

This scuffed key ring was the one she lost in Garrett's cabin on the yacht.

The key that fit in her old lock.

The one he'd carried around in his pocket for weeks.

Somehow, it had ended up in her possession all over again.

Garrett himself had to have made the switch on her. But when? In the limo, most likely, when her purse spilled. No wonder he was asking her if she'd been out yesterday. Had she gone out, she wouldn't have been able to get back in with this old key. He must have sat around all day Sunday, patiently waiting for her to realize the jig was up.

He was patiently standing by now as she connected the dots, casually holding her new key in his extended palm. Snatching it away, she unlocked her door. He was right on her as she stepped inside, as though fearful she might try to ditch him.

"So…" She teetered around, trying to keep her wobbly knees from knocking.

His black brows rose. "'So,' is all you have to say to me?"

"Well, I could accuse you of being a key stealer."

"Yes," he half roared. "And you are a heart stealer, *Flame.*"

Her voice grew small. "What put you on to me? Where did I slip up?"

"I will ask some questions first."

"Fine." She breathed shallowly, trying to conceal a shudder. The overwhelming implications of his discovery were beginning to hit. He actually knew what she'd done. Realized just to what extent she'd manipulated him. What was he going to do with her?

"First off, why did you do it, Shari?"

"Well, literacy is a very worthy cause—"

He cut her short with a growl. "Knock off the double-talk."

"All right." She sagged a little. "I've always had a yen for you since school. You were so much older then, so unattainable. I dreamed of having you."

"At that age!" He was mortified.

"Not having you like that. Back then I only wished I could go with you to your senior prom. And get a kiss or two." She sighed hard. "It's your fault you look so lethal in a tuxedo."

"Don't you dare blame me."

Her face crinkled knowingly. "C'mon, you know that much about yourself."

"Okay, I do look decent in formal wear," he admitted. "But that's as far as my responsibilities go. How did you go from innocently dreaming of the prom to luring me into a sex trap?"

"My fantasies matured right along with me," she explained matter-of-factly. "Naturally I never thought I'd have the chance to act them out, but then along came the brochure for the auction, with you in it. Garrett McNamara, up for bid. My imagination went wild."

"No argument there." Garrett shook his head ruefully, overwhelmed by the power of her feelings. How much it must have meant to her to finally be the one in the driver's seat, to bid for him absently, with her dessert fork of all things!

Just as exhilarating must have been the show she'd put on for his associates, his mother. They fussed, they praised. For once Shari was on top, in the limelight. "I'm beginning to get the big picture," he admitted. "First loves, first crushes can be powerful."

"I didn't mean to cause you any trouble. Naturally the key ring loss was accidental. After that, events started spinning out of my grasp."

"I've had one wild ride, that's for sure."

"Your search turned my life upside down, too, you

know," she said defensively. "I was so nervous, scared that you or your mother was going to unmask me at any given moment. Humiliate me with a public rejection."

He paced around. "If only you'd confided in me."

"And risk your disappointment? I was feeling too fragile to try. But you have to admit, I did my best to bring closure to it all—deliberately fell into the trap at Lily's."

"You call a joyride like that closure?"

"Passions did get out of hand," she conceded, blushing. "Way out of hand."

He closed in on her, squeezing her upper arms, searching her face urgently. "But what a double treat, knowing I had the perfect fantasy woman for me, you and Flame all in one."

An eagerness danced in her eyes behind her glasses. "So what did give me away in the end? A kiss? An embrace? Heavy breathing?"

"First of all, I have to give Peters credit for helping me see you realistically," he admitted. "After our quarrel at my place, he suggested my biggest mistake was viewing you through Dylan's overprotective eyes as the girl you used to be.

"Peters was proven right. There you were, sexy, attractive, showing a hesitant interest in me, and I couldn't quite see you for the well-rounded woman you'd become. I wanted to commit to you but couldn't get past my attraction to Flame. I'm a one-woman man, so this tug-of-war between two women was very confusing.

"After our quarrel, it seemed best to step back, gain some equilibrium. By the time Lily's party rolled around, I was prepared to take a long, hard look at the two of you in the same room."

"But I could only be in one place at one time," she reasoned, "so Flame got the nod."

"I admit I was glad to have another clear chance at Flame, to see if she affected me as deeply as you did on an emotional level." He drew her closer, nuzzling her fragrant hair. "But then the incredible happened, honey. I took Flame in my arms for that first waltz and we began to move together in perfect harmony, like the first time on the yacht and, as it happens, like you and I did at Lily's." He grinned.

"All at once I realized that dancing could be the metaphorical key to the mystery. If I closed my eyes and let my mind drift, I couldn't tell whether I was dancing with Shari or Flame.

"But I'd noticed that before, so I wasn't totally convinced even then," he confided. "It seemed so... impossible. But afterward, when you were waiting for me in the limo, tender and exotic all at once, the images of Shari and Flame merged again into one lovely, unpredictable enchantress.

"As we rode along I started putting other puzzle pieces together, like your lost key, the way you rippled your hair, your supposedly spendthrift ways. Soon there was no doubt that I was doubly gone on the same woman."

Shari sighed contentedly. "I'm glad you knew who I was when we made love a second time."

"Oh, yes." He grinned wickedly. "And I humbly apologize for ever mistaking you for inexperienced."

She frowned slightly then. "It was a dirty trick, though, lying in wait, hoping for a chance to mess with my keys."

"Your evening bag spilled by chance. I couldn't resist the idea."

"And you expected me to come back here and be horrified when I figured out your switch."

"I hoped you'd feel just a smidgen of the embarrassment I was feeling as I reviewed the big chase for my fantasy lover. Then I hoped you'd call me and we'd have a chuckle about it. But nothing happened."

"Dylan was in my apartment early Sunday morning

after the party, and I never went out after that, so naturally I didn't notice the key switch." She lightly pounded his chest. "Surprise, surprise, you are a sneaky fiend."

"That makes us a perfect match, I'd say." Crushing her against him, Garrett dipped his mouth to hers and kissed her deeply. "I love you so much, whatever name you want to call yourself."

"And I've always loved you."

"Now that we know everything between us fits down to the dead bolts, shall we plan our future?"

She looped her arms around his neck possessively. "Exactly what do you have in mind?"

"Marriage of course. You know I'm ready to settle down."

"Oh, Garrett. Can you imagine this shop girl being taken seriously as a bona fide McNamara?" Breathless, she rested back on her heels.

"I'm part of the shop now, too. A shop guy."

"However will Gwen take it?"

"Do you care?"

"Sure. She could make things miserable."

"Not a chance. All the excitement surrounding my mystery bidder has brought out the best in my mother. She's actually loosened her standards just a wee bit, opened her heart a crack."

"But she won't take my masquerade in the spirit it was intended."

Garrett chuckled at the notion. "That much is true. She'd come off as the ultimate fool after the way she shunned you and adored your alter ego. It would be downright humiliating."

"I suppose we could keep the truth from her," Shari suggested.

"At least for a while," Garrett said cheerily. "We'll save it for a delicious someday, when she is behaving impossibly with our children."

She slipped a finger along his throat. "So, who do you love most, Garrett? Shari or Flame?"

Cupping her chin, he surveyed her. "I think you're ninety percent Shari, aren't you?"

"Yes, I suppose. Flame is untamed, impractical, bold and selfish."

"True. But there's no point in cruelly shutting her away in some closet for her sins. Seems best to keep her locked in our bedroom for special occasions."

Shari smiled coyly. "I think she should be allowed out to join us on our honeymoon, too, say for a cruise aboard the *Temptation?*"

He pretended to be scandalized. "Why, you reckless minx."

"I'm only being practical. I haven't begun to get my money's worth out of that red beaded dress."

"At the rate we peel that thing off, I predict you never will...."

Look for Dylan's story from Temptation
in November 1999.

#753 OH, BABY!

Dylan Johnson is shocked—and delighted—when high
school sweetheart Allison Walker reappears in his
life...with a beautiful baby in tow. He is determined to
have the last word with Allison. But it won't be a
warm and fuzzy one!

If you enjoyed what you just read,
then we've got an offer you can't resist!

Take 2 bestselling love stories FREE!

Plus get a FREE surprise gift!

Clip this page and mail it to Harlequin Reader Service®

IN U.S.A.
3010 Walden Ave.
P.O. Box 1867
Buffalo, N.Y. 14240-1867

IN CANADA
P.O. Box 609
Fort Erie, Ontario
L2A 5X3

YES! Please send me 2 free Harlequin Temptation® novels and my free surprise gift. Then send me 4 brand-new novels every month, which I will receive months before they're available in stores. In the U.S.A., bill me at the bargain price of $3.12 plus 25¢ delivery per book and applicable sales tax, if any*. In Canada, bill me at the bargain price of $3.57 plus 25¢ delivery per book and applicable taxes**. That's the complete price and a savings of over 10% off the cover prices—what a great deal! I understand that accepting the 2 free books and gift places me under no obligation ever to buy any books. I can always return a shipment and cancel at any time. Even if I never buy another book from Harlequin, the 2 free books and gift are mine to keep forever. So why not take us up on our invitation. You'll be glad you did!

142 HEN CNEV
342 HEN CNEW

Name	(PLEASE PRINT)	
Address	Apt.#	
City	State/Prov.	Zip/Postal Code

* Terms and prices subject to change without notice. Sales tax applicable in N.Y.
** Canadian residents will be charged applicable provincial taxes and GST.
All orders subject to approval. Offer limited to one per household.
® are registered trademarks of Harlequin Enterprises Limited.

TEMP99   ©1998 Harlequin Enterprises Limited

HARLEQUIN *Duets* ™

2 new full-length novels by
2 great authors in
1 book for 1 low price!

**Buy any Harlequin Duets™ book
and SAVE $1.00!**

SAVE $1.00

when you purchase any

 HARLEQUIN

Duets ™ **book!**

Offer valid May 1, 1999, to October 31, 1999.

Retailer: Harlequin Enterprises Ltd. will pay the face value of this coupon plus 8.0¢ if submitted by the customer for this specified product only. Any other use constitutes fraud. Coupon is nonassignable, void if taxed, prohibited or restricted by law. Consumer must pay any government taxes. Valid in U.S. only. Mail to: Harlequin Enterprises Ltd., P.O. Box 880478, El Paso, TX 88588-0478 U.S.A.

Non NCH customers–for reimbursement submit coupons and proofs of sale directly to: Harlequin Enterprises Ltd., Retail Sales Dept., 225 Duncan Mill Rd., Don Mills (Toronto), Ontario, Canada M3B 3K9.

Printed in Canada 9/98

HDUETC-U

 HARLEQUIN®
Makes any time special.™

**Coupon expires
October 31, 1999.**

5 65373 00051 9 (8100) 1 06254

Look us up on-line at: http://www.romance.net

HDUETC-U

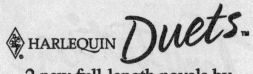

HARLEQUIN *Duets*™

2 new full-length novels by
2 great authors in
1 book for 1 low price!

**Buy any Harlequin Duets™ book
and SAVE $1.00!**

SAVE $1.00

when you purchase any

HARLEQUIN *Duets*™ book!

Offer valid May 1, 1999, to October 31, 1999.

Printed in Canada 9/98

Retailer: Harlequin Enterprises Ltd. will pay the face value of this coupon plus 10.25¢ if submitted by the customer for this specified product only. Any other use constitutes fraud. Coupon is nonassignable, void if taxed, prohibited or restricted by law. Consumer must pay any government taxes. Valid in Canada only. Mail to: Harlequin Enterprises Ltd., P.O. Box 3000, Saint John, New Brunswick, Canada E2L 4L3.
Non NCH customers–for reimbursement submit coupons and proofs of sale directly to: Harlequin Enterprises Ltd., Retail Sales Dept., 225 Duncan Mill Rd., Don Mills (Toronto), Ontario, Canada M3B 3K9.

HARLEQUIN®
Makes any time special.™

HDUETC-C

**Coupon expires
October 31, 1999.**

Look us up on-line at: http://www.romance.net   HDUETC-C

COMING NEXT MONTH